Arkady Strugatsky, Boris Strugatsky

FAR RAINBOW

Fredonia Books
Amsterdam, The Netherlands

Far Rainbow

by
Arkady Strugatsky
Boris Strugatsky

ISBN: 1-4101-0668-3

Copyright © 2004 by Fredonia Books

Fredonia Books
Amsterdam, The Netherlands
http://www.fredoniabooks.com

"We all know what Rainbow is," began Lamondois. "Rainbow is a planet colonized by science and designed for physical experiments."

Robert turned quickly. His knees went weak. He saw on the visiplate the ugly mat helmet and the round unblinking eyes of Camille.

"I haven't got much time," Camille was saying. "Evacuate the whole northern area immediately. Immediately! Behind the Liu-Wave there's a Wave of a new type. Here's the..." The screen went dark.

"How are things in the next world?" asked Gorbovsky.

"It's dark there," said Camille. "Today I died and was ressurected three times. Each time it was terribly painful."

"Three times," repeated Gorbovsky. "A record. Camille, tell me the truth. Are you human? Tell me. I shan't be able to tell anyone now."

Camille thought for a moment.

"I don't know," he said. "I'm the last of the 'Baker's Dozen'."

1

Tanya's palm, warm and slightly rough, lay across his eyes and nothing else existed for him. He was conscious of the bitter salt smell of the dust, the prairie birds were chirping sleepily, and the dry grass pricked and tickled the back of his neck. It was hard and uncomfortable lying there and his neck chafed unbearably, but he made no move, listening to Tanya's quiet even breathing. He was smiling and was glad of the darkness, for his smile was foolish and self-satisfied to a degree.

In another place and another time came the squealing of the laboratory alarm on its tower. Let it. It wasn't the first time. On an evening like this all sirens and alarms belonged to another time and another place.

"Robby," whispered Tanya. "Do you hear?"

"Not a thing," mumbled Robert.

He blinked so that his eyelashes tickled her palm. Everything was far away and unnecessary. Patrick, perpetually dazed from lack of sleep, was far away, Malayev the Icy Sphinx was far away. Their whole world of bustle and abstruse argument, never ending dissatisfaction and worry, all that nonsensual world where people despised the obvious and were only glad of the incomprehensible, where they forgot they were men and women—it was all so very far away.... Here there was only the nocturnal steppe, empty prairie for hundreds of miles around; it had swallowed up the hot day and was now warm, dark and full of exciting perfumes.

The alarm went again.

"Again," said Tanya.

"Let it. I'm not here. I'm dead. The moles have eaten me. I'm happy here. I love you. I don't want to go anywhere. What for? Would you?"

7

"Don't know."

"That's because you don't love enough. Those who love enough never go anywhere."

"Theory," said Tanya.

"Not theory, practice. As a practical scientist, I ask you: Why should I suddenly get up and go somewhere? One must know how to love. You don't. You can only discuss love. You don't like love, you only like talking about it. Am I nattering too much?"

"Terribly."

He took her hand from his eyes and placed it on his lips. Now he could see the sky, streaked with cloud, and the red identification lights on the girders of the sixty-foot tower.

The signal was going all the time now and Robert could imagine Patrick angrily pressing the button, his thick lips pouting in annoyance.

"I'll switch you off right now," said Robert indistinctly. "Tanik, do you want it to stop for ever? Let everything be for ever. We'll have our love for ever and that thing'll be quiet for evermore."

In the dark he could see her face—light with huge shining eyes. She took her hand away and said:

"Come on, I'll talk to him. I'll tell him I'm a hallucination. Hallucinations always happen at night."

"He never has hallucinations, he's that kind—he could never deceive himself."

"I'll tell you what sort of person he is, shall I? I love guessing peoples' characters by the way they signal on the visiplate. He's stubborn, bad-tempered and tactless. And he wouldn't for the world be caught sitting out with a woman in the steppe at night—right? I can see right through him. The only thing he knows about the night time is that it's dark."

"No," said the fair-minded Robert. "You're right about

sitting out with a woman, but really he's kind, and gentle and a bit of a slowcoach even."

"I don't believe it," said Tanya. "Just listen." They listened. "Does that sound like a slowcoach? He's a man firm in intention, as Horace says."

"Really? I'll tell him."

"Tell him. Go and tell him."

"What, now?"

"Straight away."

Robert got up but Tanya remained where she was, arms clasping her knees.

"Kiss me first, anyway," she demanded.

In the lift he stood for several minutes with his forehead pressed to the cold wall, his eyes were closed and he was smiling. He kept touching his lips with his tongue. His mind was a complete blank except for an exultant incoherent voice that kept shouting: "She loves.... Me! ... Me! ... It's me she loves! ... Damn it all. Me! ..." Then he realized that the lift had stopped long ago and started looking for the door. He couldn't find it straight away and the lab seemed to be very full of furniture: he knocked over chairs, shifted tables and walked into cupboards before he realized that he'd forgotten to put the light on Laughing out loud he felt for the switch and pulled an armchair to the visiplate.

When Patrick's sleepy face appeared on the screen Robert greeted him creerfully:

"Evenin', piglet! What's keeping you awake, tom-tit, o wagtail mine?"

Patrick looked at him, taken aback, blinking his reddened eyelids.

"What are you staring at, doggie? Hooting away, tearing me away from important business and now you've got nothing to say!"

Patrick opened his mouth at last:

"You had. . . . You. . ." he smote his forehead with his fist and his face looked a question. "Eh?"

"Yes indeed!" shouted Robert. "Loneliness! Angst! Oh yes—and hallucinations, I nearly forgot!"

"You're joking of course?" asked Patrick seriously.

"Never! No joking on the job! Anyway, pay no attention and get on with it."

Patrick blinked uncertainly.

"I don't understand," he confessed.

"Wake up there, Patrick!" said Robert enjoying the other's discomfiture. "It's the emotions, Patrick! Get it? . . . How can I simplify it so's you can understand. . . . Well, incomplete algorithmic perturbations in super-complex logical systems. Got it now?"

"Mmmm," said Patrick. He scratched his chin with his finger, concentrating. "Why am I calling you, Rob? Well there's a leakage somewhere. Maybe it isn't a leak and maybe it is. In any case check the ulmotrons. The Wave's funny today. . . ."

Robert stared wildly out of the window. He'd completely forgotten about the eruption. So he was sitting here because of the eruptions and not because Tanya was here. Somewhere out there was a Wave.

"Why don't you say something?" asked Patrick patiently.
"I'm seeing how the Wave's getting on," said Robert crossly.

Patrick goggled.

"You can see the Wave?"

"Me? What're you talking about?"

"You just said you were looking. . . ."

"Yes I'm looking!"

"Well?"

"Look, what do you want me to do?"

Patrick's eyes grew bleary again.

"I don't follow you," he said. "What were we talking about? Yes! Check the ulmotrons right away."

"Do you know what you're saying? How can I check the ulmotrons?"

"Somehow," said Patrick. "Maybe, switch them on.... We're in a right mess. I'll explain in a minute.... Today at the Institute we sent off a mass towards Earth.... Anyway, you know all that." Patrick waved his spread fingers in front of the visiplate. "We expected a full-force Wave and all we're registering is a sort of weak fountain. You follow me? This weak fountain, like...." He moved up to his visiplate which now showed only a huge eye, dim with fatigue. The eye went on blinking. "Do you follow?" the loudspeaker roared deafeningly. "Our apparatus is registering a quasi-null field. The Jung counter shows minimum... we can ignore that.... The ulmotron fields are overlapping so the resonating surface lies in the focal hyperplane, you see? The quasi-null field is twelve-component and the receiver reduces it to the six even components... so the focus is six-component...."

Robert thought of Tanya waiting patiently below for him. Patrick went bumbling on, moving back and forth in front of the receiver so that his voice alternately roared out and receded to a whisper; Robert as usual soon lost the thread of his arguments. He nodded, screwed up his forehead, raised his eyebrows and then lowered them, and took in exactly nothing; he thought guiltily of Tanya sitting there below with her chin on her knees, waiting for him to finish his urgent and esoteric conversation with the planet's leading null-physicists, while he propounded his own highly original point of view of the problem which had forced them to trouble him so late at night, and waited till the leading null-physicists, wagging their heads in amazement, entered that opinion in their notebooks....

Here Patrick stopped and looked at him with an odd

expression. Robert knew that look well, it had followed him all his life. Many people—men and women—had looked at him like that. At first they looked at him without excitement or even with affection, then expectantly, then with curiosity but sooner or later the time came when they began to look at him like this. And every time he was at a loss as to what to do, how to behave and how to conduct himself in future.

He decided to risk it.

"You're right at that," he pronounced worriedly, "but it needs thinking right through."

Patrick dropped his eyes.

"Think it through, then," he said, smiling awkwardly. "And check the ulmotrons, please, don't forget."

The screen went dark, all was quiet. Robert sat, bent forward, his hands clasping the cool rough elbow-rests. Somebody had once said that a fool who realized he was a fool ceased to be one by the very fact of his realization. Maybe that's how it used to be. A spoken stupidity remains a stupidity all the same, and it seems I can't do anything else. I'm a really interesting person: everything I say is stale, all my thoughts—banal, everything I do has been done two hundred years ago. I'm not just a thick-head, I'm a rare type, a museum piece, like a Cossack hetman's staff. He recalled how old Nechiporenko had once looked thoughtfully into Robert's dedicated eyes and stated: "My dear Sklyarov, you've got a god-like physique. And gods, if I may say so, have no place in science...."

Something ripped. Robert caught his breath and stared in amazement at the piece of the elbow-rest clenched in his fist.

"Yes," he said aloud, "that's something I can do. Patrick couldn't do it. Nor could Nechiporenko. Only me."

He placed the piece on the table and walked over to the window. Outside it was dark and sultry. Should I leave before I am thrown out? What'll I do without them though? And without that marvellous feeling that maybe today, at last, the invisible, impenetrable envelope in my brain will burst and I'll be like them, understanding them as soon as they open their mouths, and I'll suddenly see in a fog of logico-mathematical symbols something absolutely new and Patrick'll clap me on the shoulder and say beaming: "That's marvellous! How did you do it?" Malayev will have to squeeze something out: "That took brains... not obvious, that...." And I'll start to feel some self-respect.

"Freak," he muttered.

The ulmotrons had to be checked, Tanya could sit and watch how it was done. A good job she hadn't seen his face when the screen had gone blank.

"Tanya, darling," he called through the window.

"Hello?"

"Tanik, you know, last year Roger carved his 'Youth of the World' with me as a model?"

Tanya, after a pause, said softly:

"Wait a minute, I'll come up to you."

Robert knew that the ulmotrons were alright, he could feel it. He decided nevertheless to check everything that could be checked under laboratory conditions, firstly to regain mental equilibrium after the talk with Patrick and secondly because he was good at working with his hands and enjoyed it. It always diverted him and for a while it would give him that wonderful feeling of personal worth and significance without which life isn't worth living these days. Tanya, like the sweet, tactful person she was, sat quietly some distance from him, then silently began to help him. At three o'clock in the morning, Patrick rang again. Robert told him there was no leakage. Patrick was downcast. He snuffled in front of the screen for a bit, working something

13

out on a wad of paper, then he rolled the paper up into a tube and put his usual rhetorical question, "And what do we make of that, Rob?"

Robert glanced sideways at Tanya, who had just come out of the shower and was sitting sideways from the visiplate; he replied cautiously that he saw nothing special in it. "The usual, ordinary fountain," he said, "there was one like that after the null-transmission yesterday. Last week as well." Then he thought for a while and added that the intensity of the fountain would correspond approximately to a hundred grammes of transported material. Patrick said nothing, and it seemed to Robert that he was wavering. "The mass is what matters," said Robert. He glanced at the Jung counter and repeated, this time with complete confidence, "Yes, a hundred to a hundred and fifty grammes. How much did they send today?" "Twenty kilos," Patrick answered. "Ah, twenty kilos... then it doesn't work out." Then he had a brainwave: "What formula did you use to work out the intensity?" he asked. "Drambe," replied Patric indifferently. Robert had expected this: the Drambe formula estimated intensity pretty well. Robert, however, had had for a long time his own universal formula for the measurement of the intensity of material ejected during eruptions. He had tested it very carefully and even written it out and enclosed it in a colourful border.

Now, it seemed, the time had come to demonstrate all its advantages to Patrick.

Robert was just picking up his pencil, when Patrick swam off the screen. Robert waited, biting his lip. Somebody inquired, "You going to switch off?" Patrick made no reply. Karl Hoffmann came up to the screen, nodded pleasantly but absently in Robert's direction and called out to the side: "Patrick, have you finished talking?" Patrick's voice muttered somewhere far off, "Can't understand this. We'll

14

have to go into this really thoroughly." "I said have you finished speaking?" repeated Hoffmann. "Yes, man, yes," responded Patrick irritatedly. Whereupon Hoffmann, with a guilty smile, said: "Sorry, Robby, we're going to bed here. I'll switch off, eh?"

Gritting his teeth till his ears crackled, Robert placed the sheet of paper in front of him and with deliberate slowness copied out the fateful formula several times, shrugged his shoulders and said cheerfully:

"So I thought. That's sorted out, then. Now coffee."

He despised himself to such an extent that he sat in front of the crockery cupboard till he felt he had a grip on his facial expression.

"You do the coffee, alright?" said Tanya.

"Why me?"

"You make it, I'll watch."

"What do you mean?"

"I like watching you at work. You work very economically. You never make an unnecessary movement."

"Like a servo mechanism," he said, pleased nevertheless.

"No, not like a robot. You work like a perfectionist and it's a joy to watch anything perfect."

" 'Youth of the World'," he muttered. He was pink with pleasure.

He set out the cups and rolled the table over to the window. They sat down and he poured. Tanya sat sideways to him, her legs crossed. She was marvellously beautiful, again that puppy-like feeling of surprise and panic took hold of him.

"Tanya," he said, "this can't be, you're a hallucination." She smiled.

"Laugh if you want to. I know I look miserable. What can I do? I just want to tuck my head under your arm and wag my tail; then you'd slap my back and say, 'down, silly, down!...'"

15

"Down, silly, down!" said Tanya.

"And my back?"

"That comes later. Head under arms comes later too."

"Okay, later. What about now? Shall I make a sollar fo myself? Or a muzzle?"

"Not a muzzle," said Tanya.

"Why not a muzzle, pray?"

"I like you better without one."

"Auditory hallucination," said Robert. "How can yo possibly like me?"

"You've got nice legs."

His legs were Robert's weak point. They were strong bu too thick. Karl Hoffmann had modelled the legs for th "Youth of the World".

"I thought so," said Robert. He drained his cold coffee a a gulp. "Then I'll tell you why I love you. I'm selfish. Per haps I'm the last selfish man in the world. I love you be cause you're the only person who can put me in a goo mood."

"That's my job," said Tanya.

"A noble calling! The only trouble is everybody else ge put in a good mood as well, old and young. Especial young. Complete outsiders. With normal legs."

"Thank you, Robby."

"That last time at School, I noticed one little la Valya...or Varya, the tow-headed freckled one with th green eyes. That Varya dared to look at you with thos green eyes of his...it made my hands itch."

"Jealousy of a barefaced egoist."

"Of course it was jealousy."

"And now think how jealous he was."

"Wh-a-t?"

"Think how he looked at you. The six-foot 'Youth of th World', athlete, and a null-physicist to boot carrying th teacher over his shoulder, she melting with love...."

Robert chuckled happily.

"How could that be? We were alone then!"

"We're never alone in the school."

"Y-e-es, that's true," drawled Robert. "I remember those days, I remember. Pretty teachers and us fifteen-year-old boobies.... I went as far as throwing flowers in through the windows. Do you get much of that?"

"Lots," said Tanya thoughtfully, "especially with the girls. They develop earlier. And we've got spacemen and heroes as teachers there...it's a problem alright."

A problem, thought Robert, and she's glad of it, of course, they all love problems. It's a marvellous excuse for them to go breaking walls down. They spend their lives breaking down one wall after another.

"Tanya," he said, "what's a fool?"

"An insult," answered Tanya.

"What else?"

"A sick man who can't be cured."

"That's not a fool," Robert objected, "that's a malingerer."

"They're not my words. It's a Japanese saying: 'There's no medicine that will cure a fool.' "

"Ah, a lover's a fool as well then. The lover is sick, he's incurable. You've consoled me."

"You're not in love surely?"

"I'm incurable."

The clouds parted revealing the starry night. It would soon be morning.

"Look, there's the sun," said Tanya.

"Where?" asked Robert without particular enthusiasm.

Tanya put out the light and sat on his lap. She put her cheek close to his and pointed.

"See those four bright stars? That's Coma Berenices. To the left of the top one, faint as faint. That's where you and I were born, girls, me first, you next. It's our sun. Little Olga was born here on Rainbow, but her parents were born over there. Next year we're all going there for our summer holidays."

"Oh, Tatyana Alexandrovna," squealed Robert, "are we really going? Whee!" He kissed her cheek. "We'll all fly, we'll all fly! On a Sigma-D spaceship! Oh, can I take my doll? And Varya's kissing me, ooh!" He kissed her again.

She put her arms round his neck.

"My girls don't play with dolls."

Robert lifted her in his arms, rose and carefully negotiated the table. Only then did he notice, in the dim green light of the instruments, a lanky figure in the chair before the control panel. He startled and came to a halt.

"I think we could have the light on now," said the figure and Robert knew at once who it was.

"Gooseberry's arrived," said Tanya. "Put me down, Rob."

She broke from him and bent down to look for her fallen slipper.

"You know something, Camille," began Robert in exasperation.

"I know," said Camille.

"It's marvellous," said Tanya, wriggling into her shoe. "I'd never have believed the density of the population here's one person to a million square kilometres. Want some coffee?"

"No, thank you," said Camille.

Robert put on the light. Camille, as usual, was sitting in a most uncomfortable and ugly posture. As usual, he was wearing a white plastic helmet which covered his forehead and ears. As usual, his face expressed an indulgent boredom and his round, unblinking eyes were innocent both of curiosity and embarrassment. Screwing up his eyes against the light, Robert asked him:

"You haven't been here long?"

"Not long. And I didn't watch you or hear what you were saying."

18

"Thank you, Camille," said Tanya gaily. She was combing her hair. "You're tact itself."

"Only lazy people are tactless," said Camille.

Robert flared up.

"Anyway, Camille, what are you doing here? And do you have to keep appearing like a ghost? It gets on people's nerves."

"I'll answer that in order," remarked Camille calmly. That was a habit of his, too, to answer in order. "I came here because an eruption was due. You very well know, Robby," he closed his eyes in sheer boredom, "I come here every time an eruption starts in front of your post. Apart from that," he opened his eyes and stared at the instruments for some time in silence, "apart from that, I like you, Robby."

Robert glanced sideways at Tanya. She was listening intently, her comb still lifted.

"As touches my habits," went on Camille dully, "they're strange. Everybody's habits are strange. Only one's own habits seem natural."

"Camille," said Tanya unexpectedly, "how much is six hundred and eighty-five multiplied by three million eight hundred thousand and fifty-three?"

To his huge amazement, Robert saw a ghost of a smile appear on Camille's face. It was a horrid sight. A Jung counter might smile like that.

"A lot," answered Camille. "Something round three thousand million."

"Strange," sighed Tanya.

"What's strange?" asked Robert stupidly.

"A bit out in accuracy," explained Tanya. "Camille, why don't you have a cup of coffee?"

"No, thank you. I don't like coffee."

"Then I'm off. It's four hours flying to the school. Will you see me downstairs, Robik?"

Robert nodded, glancing at Camille in irritation. Camille was examining the Jung counter. As if he were looking into a mirror.

As usual on Rainbow, the sun rose into an absolutely clear sky. It was a small white sun with a triple corona. The night wind had dropped and it was stuffier than ever. The yellow-brown prairie with the odd outcropping of salt here and there seemed lifeless. Shimmering, misty hillocks of evaporation rose up above the salt flats.

Robert closed the window and turned on the air-conditioner, then he slowly and artistically repaired his elbow-rest. Camille walked about the lab softly and noiselessly, gazing out of the north window. Apparently he was quite insensible to the heat; Robert felt hot just looking at him, his thick white coat, long white trousers and his round shining helmet. Null-physicists used to wear helmets like that once upon a time during experiments to guard against radiation.

Ahead lay a full day of duty, twelve hours under a hot sun beating down on the roof, until the eruptions had resolved and all the effects of yesterday's experiment had disappeared. Robert had thrown off his coat and trousers and worked in shorts. The conditioner was working full blast and there was nothing else to do.

It would have been nice to splash a bit of liquid air onto the floor. There was some liquid air but not much and it was needed for the generator. He would have to suffer, thought Robert resignedly. He sat down again in front of the instruments. How marvellously cool it was in the armchair and at any rate it wouldn't stick to his body!

When it came to it, the most important thing was to be in one's place and my place is here. I carry out my small duties as well as anyone else. After all, it's not my fault that I'm not capable of anything greater. Anyway it's not even the point whether I'm in my place or not. I just can't leave even if I wanted to. I'm chained to these people, for all they get on my nerves so much, as well as to the great attempt I understand so little.

He remembered how he had been stunned while still at school by the daring of it: the instantaneous transmission of material objects across the deeps of space. The idea had been put forward in the teeth of everything, against all previously held theories of absolute space, space-time, Kappa space.... They used to call it then "penetrating the Riemann fold". Then "hyperfiltration", "sigma-filtration", "null-twist". Finally, null-transportation or "null-T" for short. "Null-T installation". "Null-T problems". "Null-T tester". "Null-physicist". "Where d'you work?" "I'm a null-physicist." A glance of astonished admiration. "Listen, tell me just what is null-physics? I can't understand it." "That makes two of us." Y-e-s, well....

Something could have been said of course. The staggering metamorphosis of the elementary conservation laws when the null-transmission of a small cube of platinum on Rainbow's equator caused at the poles—always at the poles, for some reason—great geysers of degenerate material, blinding fiery fountains, and the terrible black Wave, fatal to everything living....

And the fierce struggles, frightening in their intensity, between the null-physicists themselves, the incomprehensible split between people of remarkable ability, who supposedly worked shoulder to shoulder but were in fact so at odds that even if Etienne Lamondois stubbornly continued work on null-transport problems, the younger school reckoned that the Wave, the new jinnee that science had let out of the bottle, was the most important factor in the whole null-problem.

And the fact that for some reason, as yet undiscovered,

null-transport could not transmit living beings, and the dogs, the eternal martyrs, arrived at the receiving point as heaps of organic slag.... And the null-riders, "the roaring ten", headed by the great Gaba, those fit supertrained lads, hanging about on Rainbow for three years on constant readiness to enter the starting chamber in place of the dogs....

"Soon we'll be parting, Robby," said Camille suddenly.

Robert, on the verge of day-dreaming, shook himself. Camille was standing with his back to him by the north window.

Robert sat up straight and passed his hand over his face. It came away wet.

"Why?" he asked.

"Science. All this is hopeless, Robby."

"I've known that for long enough," muttered Robert.

"For you all, science is a labyrinth. Dead ends, dark corners, sudden turnings. You can't see anything except the walls. You don't know anything about the final aim either. You said that your aim was to go on to the end of eternity, in other words there simply is no aim. The measure of your success isn't the distance to the finish but the distance from the start. You're lucky you can't visualize abstractions. Aim, eternity, endlessness—they're all just words to you. Abstract philosophical categories. They mean nothing to you in your daily life. But if you could see that whole labyrinth from above...."

Camille stopped. Robert waited a moment:

"And you've seen it?" he asked.

Camille made no reply and Robert decided not to press him. He sighed, sank his chin onto his fist and closed his eyes. A man talks and acts, he thought. And it's all the outward signs of processes deep in his nature. Most men have quite shallow natures and so the slightest movement below shows on the surface at once, in inane chatter for the most part, or meaningless hand gestures. With people like Camille the processes have to be very powerful to even get to the surface. If only one could get a peep inside him.... Robert had a vision of a yawning abyss with shapeless phosphorescent shadows darting about.

Nobody likes him. Everybody knows him—there isn't a man on Rainbow who doesn't know Camille—but not a soul likes the man. If I were as lonely as him I'd go out of my mind, but it seems as if Camille just isn't interested. He's always by himself. None knows where he lives. He turns up suddenly and just as suddenly vanishes. You can see his white helmet in the Capital or out at sea, and there are people who'll tell you that he's been seen in both places at once. It's the local folk-lore of course, but everything you hear about Camille sounds like an odd story. He has a strange way of saying "I" and "you". Nobody's seen him working but from time to time he turns up at the Council and says some pretty strange things. Sometimes he can be understood and then none can argue with him. Lamondois once said that next to Camille he felt like the stupid grandson of a wise grandfather. In general the impression was left that all the physicists on Rainbow from Etienne Lamondois to Robert Sklyarov were on one level....

Robert felt that he was close to boiling in his own sweat. He got up and headed for the shower. He stood under the icy jets until his skin was covered with goosepimples and his desire to crawl into a refrigerator and go to sleep had passed off.

When he got back to the laboratory, Camille was talking with Patrick. Patrick was screwing up his forehead and moving his lips in perplexity, and looking at Camille with an expression at once doleful and ingratiating. Camille was saying in a bored and patient way:

"Try to take all the three factors into account. All three at once. You don't need any theory here, all you need is

23

a little spatial imagination. A null-actor in subspace in both temporal coordinates. Can't you manage that?"

Patrick shook his head slowly. He was a pitiful sight. Camille waited for a moment, then shrugged and switched off the visiplate. Robert, rubbing himself down with a rough towel, said crisply:

"Why do that, Camille? It's rude. He'll be offended."

Camille shrugged once more. On him it looked as if his head, weighed down by his helmet, had sunk down into his chest and popped up again.

"Offended?" he said. "And why not?"

There was no answer to this. Robert felt instinctively that it would be useless to argue with Camille on moral principles. Camille simply wouldn't understand what he was talking about.

He hung up the towel and started on breakfast. They ate in silence. Camille contented himself with a piece of bread and jam and a glass of milk. Camille always ate sparingly Finally he said:

"Robby, do you know if the 'Arrow' has left yet?"

"Day before yesterday," said Robert.

"Day before yesterday. . . . That's bad."

"What d'you need the 'Arrow' for, Camille?"

"It's not I who needs it."

2

Gorbovsky asked Percy to stop on the outskirts of the Capital. He climbed out of the car.

"I feel like a walk," he said.

"Right you are," said Mark Falkenstein, getting out beside him.

The straight shining road was empty, the prairie spread green and yellow on either side: ahead the walls of town houses peeped out in multi-coloured patches through gaps in the lush terrestrial vegetation.

"It's too hot," protested Percy Dixon. "Bad for the heart."

Gorbovsky picked a flower from the roadside and lifted it to his face.

"I like it when it's hot," he said. "Come on, Percy. You're as fat as a pig these days."

Percy slammed the door.

"Say what you like. To tell the truth I've got heart sick of you both in the last twenty years. I'm an old man and I need a rest from your paradoxes. And I'd count it a favour if you'd stay away from me on the beach."

"You'd better visit the school, Percy," said Gorbovsky. "I don't know where it is, of course, but there you'll find children, innocent laughter, simple ways. 'Mister,' they'll shout, 'let's play piggy back!'"

"Watch the beard, though," added the grinning Mark. "They'll swing on it if you don't look out."

Percy muttered something under his breath and roared off. Mark and Gorbovsky moved over onto the path and began their slow walk into town.

"Beardy's getting on," said Mark. "We've got on his nerves already."

"What do you mean now, Mark?" said Gorbovsky. He took a recorder from his pocket. "We haven't got on his

25

nerves at all. He's tired, that's the answer. Disappointed as well. It's no joke—a man wastes twenty years on us: he wants to find out what influence space has had on us. And for some reason it hasn't had any.... Africa I want, where's my Africa? Why do all my tapes always get mixed up?"

He wandered along the path after Mark, with a flower in his teeth, running through his records and falling over his feet every thirty seconds. Finally he found Africa and the yellow-green prairie echoed to the beat of the tom-tom. Mark looked over his shoulder.

"Switch that rubbish off, will you?" he asked in a tone of disgust.

"What d'you mean, rubbish? Just the thing."

The tom-toms hammered on.

"Well, turn it down at least."

Gorbovsky did so.

"Bit more, please."

Gorbovsky pretended to turn it lower.

"That all right?" he asked.

"I can't imagine why I haven't smashed that thing long ago," said Mark into space.

Gorbovsky hastily turned the volume right down and put the recorder in his breast pocket.

They were walking past gaily painted houses, each one set in its clump of lilac and each one crowned with the lattice cone of its energy receiver. A ginger cat crossed the path stealthily. "Pss-pss-pss," called Gorbovsky, overjoyed. The cat took to its heels and stared out from the thick grass with wild eyes. Bees lazily hummed in the heavy air. From somewhere close at hand came a thick, resonant snore.

"It's like a big village," said Mark. "The Capital! Sleep till nine."

"Don't go on so, Mark," objected Gorbovsky. "Now I find

it very nice here. Bees . . . a cat's just run across our path . . .
what else do you want? Shall I turn the recorder up?"

"No thanks," said Mark. "I don't like lazy hamlets like
this, lazy people live in them."

"Yes, I know you," said Gorbovsky. "You want it always
to be a struggle and argument, ideas flashing, a fight if
it can be arranged but that would be too good. . . . Hey,
hang on! That nettles or something like, it's lovely. Painful though."

He sat down in front of a thick bush with large black-
striped leaves. Mark was annoyed: "What're you squatting
down there for, Leonid, have you never seen a nettle before?"

"Never. I've read about it though. Tell you what, Mark,
I'll release you from the ship . . . you've got spoiled and
spoonfed. You've forgotten how to enjoy the simple life."

"I don't know what the simple life is," said Mark. "But
all these flowery nettles and country roads and winding
little paths, Leonid, as I see it only corrupt a man. In this
world there's enough that's still to put right before you start
ooing and ahing whenever you see a cowshed."

"There are things to put right," agreed Gorbovsky. "But
there always have been and always will be. What sort of
a life is it without wrongs to right? Anyway things are alright. Listen, somebody's singing . . . despite all the troubles
of the world. . . ."

Along the road towards them came an enormous transport atomocar. Sitting on boxes in the back were several
tough young men stripped to the waist. One, oblivious of
the world, was bent over his banjo and as he twanged
furiously, his companions roared in unison:

> I need a wife, good or bad,
> As long as she's a woman
> And single.

27

The atomocar hurtled past bending the grass with a wave of hot air.

"That ought to please you, Mark," said Gorbovsky. "Nine o'clock and people already up and working. How did you like the song?"

"Not much," said Mark stubbornly.

The path made a turn to the right in order to pass round a huge concrete basin filled with dark water. The way led through chest-high yellow grass. It got cooler—up above hung the thick branches of black acacias.

"Mark," whispered Gorbovsky. "Here's a girl coming."

Mark stopped as though transfixed. Through the grass pushed a tall well-built brunette, wearing white shorts and a little jacket with the buttons missing. She was pulling a length of heavy cable behind her with obvious difficulty.

"Hello!" said Gorbovsky and Mark in unison.

The dark-haired girl stopped sharply. Her face showed alarm. Mark and Gorbovsky exchanged glances.

"Good day, young lady!" bellowed Mark.

The girl let fall the cable and looked at her feet.

"Hello," she whispered.

"I have a feeling," said Gorbovsky, "that we're intruding here."

"Want any help?" asked Mark gallantly.

The girl regarded him from beneath her lowered lashes.

"Snakes," she said suddenly.

"Where?" cried Gorbovsky, alarmed. He lifted one leg in the air.

"All over the place," explained the girl. She looked Gorbovsky over. "Did you see the dawn today?" she inquired ingratiatingly.

"We've seen the sun come up four times today," said Mark carelessly.

The girl frowned and straightened her hair with a precisely rehearsed gesture. Mark at once introduced himself.

"Falkenstein. Mark."

"D-spaceman," added Gorbovsky.

"Oh, a D-spaceman," said the girl in an odd tone. She hoisted the cable, winked at Mark and vanished into the grass. Gorbovsky looked at Mark. Mark was following the girl with his eyes.

"Go on, Mark, go on," said Gorbovsky, "it'll look quite natural. The cable's a ton weight, the girl's not strong and you're a big tough spaceman."

Mark thoughtfully stepped on the cable. It twitched and a voice called from the grass:

"Ease out, Simeon, slacken off!"

Mark hurriedly took his foot away. They went on.

"Funny girl," said Gorbovsky, "sweet though!" "By the way, Mark, why haven't you ever got married?"

"Who to?"

"Now, now, Mark, don't be like that. Everybody knows. She's a sweet, marvellous woman. Refined, fastidious—I always reckoned you were a bit crude for her. She didn't think so though."

"Yes, well I didn't get married," said Mark unwillingly. "It just didn't turn out that way."

The path was leading them once more towards the road. On the left some tall white cisterns rose up, while dead ahead a silver spire flashed in the sun on top of the Council building. There was still nobody about.

"She was too fond of music," said Mark. "You can't take a choriola with you on every flight. Your recorder's bad enough. Percy can't stand music."

"Every flight," repeated Gorbovsky. "The whole trouble is we're too old, Mark. Twenty years ago we wouldn't have argued which was finer, love or friendship. Now it's too late. We're doomed. Anyway, don't lose hope, Mark, perhaps we'll meet some women yet who'll be worth all the rest."

"Percy won't," said Mark. "He hasn't even got any friends except us two. Percy in love. . . ."

Gorbovsky imagined Percy Dixon in love.

"He'd have made a fine father," he suggested, without conviction.

Mark frowned.

"You can't say that. Anyway a child doesn't need a good father. He needs a good teacher. And a man needs a good friend. What a woman needs is someone to love. Let's talk about something else."

The square in front of the Council was empty. The only sign of life was a big clumsy aerobus standing by the drive.

"I'd like to set eyes on Matvei again," said Gorbovsky. "Come on, Mark."

"Who's Matvei?"

"I'll introduce you. Matvei Vyazanitsyn. Matvei Sergeyevich. He's the director here. He's by way of being an old friend of mine, spaceman, scout. You're bound to remember him, Mark. No, on second thought, it'd be before your time."

"Well, alright, let's go. A social call. Turn that thing off though, not done, you know. It is the Council, after all."

The director was very glad to see them.

"Terrific!" he shouted, sitting them down in armchairs. "It's great to see you! Leonid, you're a marvel! What a bloke. Falkenstein? Mark? Of course, of course . . . why aren't you bald? Leonid distinctly told me you were bald . . . oh, no, that was Dixon. I know Dixon's got a famous beard but you can't go by that—I know plenty of bald blokes with beards as well! Anyway what am I going on about that for? Don't you find it hot here? Leonid, you look like you need a good dinner. We'll eat together ... in the meantime let me get you a drink. Orange juice, tomato juice, pomegranate ... home grown, you know! Yes, we grow our own wine on Rainbow, fancy that, eh? Well, what d'you think of it? Odd, I like it ... you try a spot, Mark? Well, I'd never have thought you a teetotaler! Ah, I see you don't drink local wines! Leonid, there's a load of questions I want to ask you. I can't think where to start and in a minute I'm going to stop being a human being and turn into a demon administrator. You've never seen one? You soon will.... I'm going to turn into a judge, chastiser and dispenser of benevolence. I shall rule, having first divided! Now I know what a poor time of it the old kings and dictators must have had! Listen, men, just don't go away, will you? I'll be up to my ears in it and you can sit and sympathize with me. Nobody sympathizes with me here.... You're okay here, aren't you? I'll just open this window a fraction, bit of fresh air.... You've got no idea, Leonid.... You can move over into the shadow there, Mark. Well, Leonid, you know wha's going on round these parts? The whole planet's in an uproar and this is the second year it's been going on...."

He collapsed into an armchair which let out a groan. He was a huge man burned black by the sun, his shaggy whiskers stuck out in front like an old tom cat. He unloosed his shirt as far as his waist and looked over his shoulder at the spacemen who were assiduously sucking the ice-cold juices through straws. His whiskers trembled and he was about to open his mouth when a thin, rather pleasant-looking woman appeared on one of the six screens in front of him at the desk. Her eyes expressed displeasure.

"Director," she said very seriously. "My name is Haggerton, you don't remember me I expect. I spoke to you about the ray barrier on Mount Alabaster. The physicists are refusing to take it down."

"What d'you mean, refusing?"

"I spoke to Rodriguez—he's the chief null up there, isn't he?—and he said you had no right to interfere in their work. . . ."

"They're pulling your leg, Ellen!" shouted Matvei. "Rodriguez is as much in charge up there as my Aunt Fanny. He repairs the robots. He understands less about null-physics than you do. I'll deal with him right now."

"Would you be so kind?"

Shaking his head, the director twiddled the nobs in front of him.

"Alabaster!" he barked. "Put Pagava on!"

"Pagava here, Matvei."

"Shota? Hello there! Why aren't you taking the barrier down?"

"I've taken it down. Why shouldn't I?"

"Ah, that's good. Tell Rodriguez, will you, to stop having people on or I'll have him sent up here! Tell him, I remember him from last time! How's your Wave getting on?"

"Well. . . ." Shota paused. "It's an interesting Wave. It's a long story, I'll tell you later."

"Well all the best!" Leaning across the arm of his chair, Matvei addressed the spacemen. "Incidentally, Leonid, that reminds me, what do your lot think about the Wave?"

"My lot where?" asked Gorbovsky coolly, sucking away at his straw. "You mean on the 'Tariel'?"

"Well what do you think about it yourself, then?"

Gorbovsky pondered.

"I don't think anything," he said. "Mark, perhaps?" He looked at the navigator without expectation.

Mark was sitting bolt upright, somehow official, holding his glass in his hand.

"If I'm not mistaken," he said, "the Wave is a sort of process to do with null-transportation. I know a bit about that. Naturally, like every spaceman, I'm interested in null-transport," he bowed slightly towards the director, "but on

32

Earth they aren't all that interested in it. I think the discrete physicists back on Earth are of the opinion that it's too specialized a problem, with an obvious practical application."

The director gave a jaundiced laugh.

"How d'you like that, Leonid?" he said. "A specialized problem! It's plain we're too far away from you on Rainbow. Everything that happens here seems unimportant as far as you are concerned. My dear Mark, that same specialized problem has been my whole life's work—and I'm not even a null-physicist! I'm worn out, I tell you! Why yesterday in this very study I stopped Aristotle and Lamondois from tearing each other apart. Now I look at my hands," here he stretched out his powerful sunburned hands in front of him, "and I'm honestly amazed there's no bites and scratches on them. There were two crowds roaring under my window, one shouting 'the Wave, the Wave'; and the other: 'null-T'. And it wasn't a scientific dispute, oh no! It was a shared apartment's squabble over the electricity bill. Well, anyway, Aristotle and his mob were trying to tear Lamondois and his mob apart because they'd taken the whole energy reserve into their hands. . . . Holy Rainbow! A year ago the two of them were going around arm in arm. One null-physicist was friend and brother to another and nobody ever thought that Forster's passion for the Wave would split the whole planet in two! What a life I've got, I tell you! There's not enough of anything, energy, equipment, nothing, and there's a battle over every tender-foot laboratory assistant. Lamondois' lot steal energy, Aristotle's people get hold of any outsiders they can lay their hands on and try to win them over to their side—tourists, mind you, who've come to Rainbow to have a rest or to write something nice about the place! The Council—the Council!!—it's turned into a battleground! I asked them to send me a book on Roman Law. . . . I read nothing but historical novels nowadays. Holy Rainbow! I'm going to organize a police force here and courts too. I'm starting to get used to a barbarous new language! Yesterday I started calling Lamondois the defendant and Aristotle the plaintiff! I can pronounce words like jurisprudence and police-presidium without batting an eyelid!"

One of the screens lit up. Two ten-year-old girls appeared. They stared round-faced at him. One was in a red dress and one was dressed in blue.

"Go on, you talk!" said red dress in a whisper.

"Why me? We agreed that you...."

"You!"

"Sneak!... Hello, Matvei Simeonovich...."

"Sergeyevich!"

"Matvei Sergeyevich, hello!"

"Hello, kids," said the director. Judging by his face, he'd forgotten something and they reminded him of it. "Hello chickens! Hello mice!"

The red and the blue glowed in unison.

"Matvei Sergeyevich, we invite you to the school to the summer fête...."

"Twelve o'clock today!"

"Eleven!"

"No, twelve!"

"I'll be there," cried the director ecstatically. "Of course I'll be there! I'll come at twelve and at eleven!..."

Gorbovsky finished his glass, poured himself a little more, then lay snuggled down into the armchair, stretching his legs out into the middle of the room. He balanced the glass on his chest. He felt pleasant and cosy.

"I'll go to the school as well," he announced. "I'm at a complete loose end. I'll give them a speech. I've never given one in my life and I'm dying to have a crack."

"The school!" the director leaned back again across the chair arm. "The school's the only place round here where there's any sort of order! Children are marvellous! They know just what you mean when you say the word 'no'.... You can't say that about our physicists, oh no! Last year they ate up two million megawatt hours. This year, fifteen already, and they've put in an estimate for another sixty. The whole trouble is they just can't understand the word 'no'...."

"We didn't reckon that word either," observed Mark.

"My dear Mark! We lived at the right time, you and I. The crisis in physics. We didn't need anything more than what we were given! Why should we? What did we have? D-processes, electronic structure.... Only a few people were working on problems of conjugate space and only on paper at that.... And now? Now we have the mad age of discrete physics, filtration theory, subspace! Holy Rainbow! These null-problems! Every bright young thing, every spindly-legged lab assistant needs thousands of megawatts for every piddling experiment he does, as well as unique equipment that you just can't get on Rainbow, and doesn't work afterwards, incidentally.... You've brought a hundred ulmotrons! Thank you very much! But they want six hundred! And energy...energy! Where can I get that from? You didn't bring us any of that! Anyway, you need that yourselves.... Kaneko and I had a word with the machine: give us the optimum strategy! Poor thing, it couldn't make head or tail of it!..."

The door was flung open and a short man dashed into the room. He was dressed with elegant neatness. Some sort of burdock was sticking up in his smoothly combed black hair and his set face showed a cold restrained fury.

"Talk of the devil..." began the director, putting out his hand.

"I'm resigning," said the newcomer, in a ringing metallic voice. "I've decided that I'm not capable of working with people any more, so I'm resigning.... Excuse me," he bowed shortly towards the spacemen. "Kaneko, energy planner for Rainbow. Former energy planner."

Gorbovsky hastily scraped his feet on the slippery floor, trying to raise himself and bow at the same time. He held the glass of juice above his head the while thus giving a fair impression of the drunken guest in Lucullus' triclinium.

"Holy Rainbow!" said the director anxiously. "What's gone wrong now?"

"Half an hour ago Simeon Galkin and Alexandra Postysheva plugged in to the zonal energy system and took all the energy for two days ahead," a tremor passed over the face of Kaneko. "The machine's programmed to deal with honest people only. I don't know of any subprogramme that can take people like Galkin and Postysheva into account. The very fact is unacceptable, though it's nothing new to us, unfortunately. I could have dealt with them myself only I'm not a judoka, or an acrobat either. And I'm not trained to look after children. I can't stand them setting traps for me.... They camouflaged their installation in a clump of bushes the other side of the gully and laid the lead right across the path. They knew very well that I'd be coming at a run to cut off an energy drain like that...." He suddenly stopped and began picking grass out of his hair.

"Where's Postysheva?" asked the director; the blood had rushed to his face. Gorbovsky sat up straight and hugged his knees in something like alarm. Mark's face showed only a keen interest in what was going on.

"She'll be here directly," Kaneko answered. "I'm as sure as you are that she's the one behind this business. I used your name to make her come here."

Matvei drew the general circuit microphone towards him and said in a soft bass:

"Attention, Rainbow. Director speaking. I know all about the energy drain. The incident is being investigated."

He got up and turned to Kaneko, placing his hand on his shoulder.

"I told you, friend," he said, a trace of guilt in his voice, "Rainbow's gone mad. Bear up, lad! I will as well. As for Postysheva, I'll roast her directly. She'll laugh on the other side of her face, you watch. . . ."

"I know," said Kaneko. "Please excuse me—I was furious. With your permission I'll be off to the spaceport. It's the worst business of all today—distributing the ulmotrons. There's a ship arrived, you know, with a load of them."

"Yes," said the director with feeling. "I know. Here," he pointed at the spacemen with his square jaw, "they're worth knowing—my friends. Leonid Andreyevich Gorbovsky, commander of the 'Tariel' and his navigator, Mark Falkenstein."

"Glad to have met you," said Kaneko, inclining his grassy head. Mark and Gorbovsky bowed in their turn.

"I shall try to keep damage to the ship to a minimum," said Kaneko unsmiling as he turned and made for the door. Gorbovsky looked after him uneasily.

The door opened in front of him and he politely stepped to one side to allow the person to enter. In the doorway stood familiar brunette in a short white jacket with the buttons missing. Gorbovsky noticed her shorts were charred through at the side and her left hand was blackened with soot. Next to her, the smart and elegant Kaneko looked like a visitor from the far future.

"Excuse me, please," said the brunette in a velvet voice. "May I come in? You sent for me, Matvei Sergeyevich?"

Kaneko turned his face away, crept round her and vanished behind the door. Matvei came back to his chair, sat down and leaned his elbows on the arm-rests. His face again darkened.

"D'you think I don't know what you're up to, Postyshe-va?..."

A pink-faced young man appeared on the screen, wearing a beret perched rakishly on the side of his head.

"Excuse me, Matvei Sergeyevich," said he smiling cheerfully. "I wanted to remind you that two sets of ulmotrons are ours."

"Wait your turn, Karl," growled Matvei.

"We're first in the queue," informed the young man.

"You'll get them first, then." Matvei was all the time looking at Postysheva, keeping his expression fierce and forbidding.

"Excuse me again, Matvei Sergeyevich, but we're very worried about the behaviour of Forster's group. I saw their truck already on its way to the spaceport."

"Don't worry, Karl," said Matvei. He couldn't help himself and broke into a smile. "Look at that, Leonid! Bloke comes and tells tales! Who? Hoffmann. Who does he tell on? Forster—his own teacher! Go on, Karl, go on. Nobody will be served out of turn!"

"Thank you, Matvei Sergeyevich," said Hoffmann. "Malayev and I are relying on you."

"Malayev and him!" said the director, raising his eyes to the ceiling.

The screen went blank and a moment later flickered on. A middle-aged man in dark glasses with some kind of auxiliary lenses fitted to the frames, was hooting discontentedly:

"Matvei, I just wanted to make sure about the ulmotrons...."

"Wait your turn," said Matvei.

The brunette sighed wearily, stared piercingly at Mark and seated herself on the edge of an armchair with every appearance of humility.

"We have authority to jump the queue," said the man in the dark glasses.

"So you'll jump the queue," said Matvei. "There's a queue of jumpers too and you're eighth on it."

The brunette, bending over gracefully, took to examining the hole in her shorts, then, licking her fingers, she wiped the soot from her elbow.

"One moment, Postysheva," said Matvei and bent over the microphone. "Attention, Rainbowl Director speaking. The ulmotrons delivered here on board 'Tariel' will be handed out in strict accordance with the decision of the Council. There will be no exceptions made. Right, Postysheva.... I brought you here to say I'm fed up with you. I've been soft with you in the past, yes, and patient. I put up with everything. You can't say I've been cruel. But Holy Rainbowl There's a limit to everything! Anyway, tell Galkin that I'm relieving you of your duties and you'll be leaving for Earth on the next ship."

Postysheva's large and lovely eyes immediately filled with tears. Mark shook his head sorrowfully. Gorbovsky became downcast. The director thrust out his jaw and looked at Postysheva.

"Too late to cry now, Alexandra," he said. "You should have thought of that earlier, when we did."

A pretty woman in a pleated skirt and blue cardigan came into the room. Her hair was cut short and a light-brown bang fell down over her eyes.

"Hello!" said she, smiling brightly. "Matvei, I'm not intruding, am I?" "Oh," she noticed Postysheva. "What's going on? Are we crying?" She put her arms round Postysheva and hugged her head to her chest. "Matvei, are you behind this? How could you? You've been nasty to her, I expect. You really are unbearable sometimes!"

The director twitched his moustaches.

"Good morning, Gina," he said. "Let go of Postysheva.

She's been punished. She's offended Kaneko unforgivably and she's been stealing energy."

"What nonsense!" exclaimed Gina. "Now don't fret, my dear! What language: 'offended', 'stealing', 'energy'! Who's she been stealing energy from? Not from the school anyway! What difference does it make which physicist wastes energy, Alya Postysheva or that awful Lamondois!"

The director rose majestically.

"Leonid, Mark," he brought out. "This is Gina Pickbridge, senior biologist on Rainbow. Gina, this is Leonid Gorbovsky and Mark Falkenstein, spacemen."

The spacemen stood up.

"Hello," said Gina. "No, I don't want to know you.... Why should two tough handsome men be so heartless? How can you just sit and look at a girl who's crying?"

"We aren't heartless!" protested Mark. Gorbovsky looked at him in astonishment. "We wanted to interfere as a matter of fact...."

"Well go on then, interfere!" said Gina.

"Now look here, people!" said the director. "I don't like this at all! Postysheva, you're free to go, so off with you. What's the matter, Gina? Let her go and say what you came for. There you are you see, she's cried all over your cardigan. Postysheva, go on, be off with you!"

Postysheva got up and went out, her face buried in her hands. Mark looked a question at Gina.

"But of course!" said she.

Mark hitched up his jacket and with a stern glance at Matvei bowed to Gina and also left the room. Matvei gave a weak wave of the hand.

"I give up," he said. "No discipline. You know what you're doing, Gina?"

"Naturally," said Gina, moving over to the table. "Alya's worth all your physics and all your energy."

"Tell that to Lamondois. Or Pagava. Or Forster. Or Kaneko, for that matter. Everybody's got his weapon, hers is tears. Anyway, that's enough of that, if you don't mind. What did you come for?"

"Yes, alright," said Gina. "I know you're as stubborn as you're nice. And that's saying something! Men are what I need. No, no." She held up a protesting palm. "It's going to be dangerous and interesting work. I've only got to lift my little finger and half your physicists will desert their masters and come running."

"If you lift your finger, their masters'll come running as well."

"Well, thank you, but I was thinking of a squid hunt. I need twenty men to chase the squids away from Pushkin shore."

Matvei sighed.

"What have they done to you?" he replied. "I haven't got anybody spare."

"Well, ten then. The squids are systematically raiding the fish-farms. What are your test men doing just now?"

Matvei came to life.

"Of course!" he said. "Gaba! Where's he now? Oh, yes, I remember.... It's okay, Gina, you'll have your ten men."

"Well, that's alright, then. I always said you were nice. I'm off to breakfast, so they can come and find me. Goodbye, dear Leonid. If you want to take part we'll be only too glad."

"Whew!" said Matvei, when the door had closed behind her. "She's a marvellous woman but I still prefer to work with Lamondois. But how do you like Mark?"

Gorbovsky smirked and poured himself another glass. He stretched blissfully in the armchair and with a murmured, "you don't mind?" he turned on his recorder. The director also lay back.

"Yes!" he mused. "Remember, Leonid—the Blind Spot.

Stanislav Pishta shouting over all the air waves.... Yes, incidentally, you know...."

"Matvei Sergeyevich," said a voice from the receiver. "Signal from the 'Arrow'."

"Read it," said Matvei, leaning forward.

" 'I am coming out onto deritrinitation. Next transmission in 40 hours time. All well. Anton.' Quality poor, Matvei Sergeyevich. There's a magnetic storm going on."

"Thank you," said Matvei. He turned to Gorbovsky with a worried look on his face. "By the way, Leonid, what's your opinion of Camille?"

"That he never takes his helmet off," said Gorbovsky. "I once asked him straight out about it, when we were out swimming. He told me straight as well!"

"Well, what do you think of him?"

Gorbovsky pondered.

"I think it's his right."

Gorbovsky didn't feel like talking about this. After listening to the tom-toms for a minute or two, he added:

"You know, Matty, somehow people think of me as being almost a friend of Camille's. Everybody asks me about him. Well, I don't like discussing it. If you want to ask anything concrete, go ahead."

"Okay," said Matvei. "Is Camille alright in the head?"

"Of course he is, he's a perfectly normal genius."

"You know, I wonder all the time: Why does he keep on prophesying? He's got this thing about predicting...."

"Well, what does he predict?"

"You know, just nothing," said Matvei. "The end of the world. The whole trouble is there's not a soul who can understand him. Anyway that's enough of that. What were we talking about?"

The screen lit up again. Kaneko appeared. His tie was round his ear.

"Matvei Sergeyevich," he said, slightly out of breath. "I'd like to check the list. You should have a copy."

"Hell, I'm sick of all this!" said Matvei. "Leonid, I'm sorry, I'll have to go."

"Of course, of course," said Gorbovsky. "I'll take a stroll over to the spaceport. See how 'Tariel' is getting on."

"Be here for dinner at two," said Matvei.

Gorbovsky finished his drink, rose and, with a feeling of profound pleasure, turned the tom-toms up full blast.

3

By ten the heat had become impossible. Salt blowing in from the baking steppe had worked itself into the cracks in every closed window. Mirages danced above the prairie. Robert had arranged two powerful ventilators by his chair and, half-reclining, was fanning himself with an old magazine. He was consoling himself with the thought that by three it would get a good deal worse. Then it would be evening at last. Camille had frozen into stillness by the north window. Their conversation had petered out.

The endless blue tape trailed out of the registrator, covered with the jagged line of the automatic recordings, the Jung counter imperceptibly filled with a deep violet light, the ulmotrons keened thinly, while behind their mirror-like windows came the flashing play of nuclear collision. The Wave was growing. Somewhere beyond the northern horizon monstrous gouts of hot poisonous dust churned in the stratosphere above invisible wastes of charred earth. . . .

The visiplate sounded bringing Robert to the alert. He thought it must be Patrick or—awful thought in this heat—Malayev. It turned out to be Tanya, however, fresh and cheerful, and it was obvious straight away it wasn't a hundred in the shade where she was. No stink from the dead steppe either. The air was sweet and clean with the scent of flowers drifting in from the beds by the incoming tide.

"How are things without me, Robik?" she asked.

"Bad," complained Robert. "It stinks. And it's hot. You're not here. I want to go to sleep more than anything but I can't drop off."

"Poor boy. . . . I dozed right off in the helicopter. I've got a hard day in front of me too. It's the summer fête—bedlam, chaos, the absolute end. . . . The boys are going mad. Are you by yourself?"

"No. Camille's here, not seeing and not hearing us. Tanik, I want to see you today. Where and when?"

"Are you off today? Let's fly south!"

"Okay, let's. Remember the café in Fisheries? We'll eat octopus and drink young wine ... iced!" Robert fetched a groan and closed his eyes. "God, how I'm going to look forward to this evening!"

"Me too...." She looked over her shoulder. "Love and kisses, Robby," she said, "I'll give you a ring."

"I'll look forward to it" was all Robert managed to say.

Camille continued to stare out of the window, his fingers linked behind his back. They were in constant motion. Camille had unusually long white flexible fingers with nails cut short. He could do fantastic things with them and Robert caught himself trying to imitate their coilings and entwinings.

"It's started," said Camille suddenly. "I advise you to come and look."

"What's started?" asked Robert. He certainly didn't feel like getting up.

"The steppe," said Camille.

Robert reluctantly got up and went over to the window. At first he saw nothing. Then he thought he was the victim of a mirage. Striving to see better he threw himself forward so that he banged his head against the pane. The steppe was moving. It was changing colour swiftly—a horrible reddish porridge was crawling across the yellow prairie. Down below under the signal tower, red and rust dots could be seen swarming among the dry stubble.

"God almighty!" exclaimed Robert. "Red rust! What are you standing there for?" He threw himself at the visiplate. "Shepherds!" he shouted. "Duty man!"

"Duty man here."

"Prairie post here! Rust coming down from the north! The whole steppe's covered with it!"

"What? Say that again. Who's speaking?"

"It's the steppe look-out here, observer Sklyarov. There's a rust coming down from the north! It's worse than the year before last! Got it? The whole steppe's teeming with it!"

"Okay ... got it ... thanks Sklyarov... that's a pity. All our stuff's in the south. What a bind... well okay...."

"Listen!" shouted Robert, "listen, get in touch with Alabaster and Greenfield. There's tons of nulls there, they'll give you a hand!"

"Right you are! Thanks, Sklyarov. Let me know as soon as the rust stops coming on."

Robert dashed to the window again. The rust was coming on like a wave, the grass had disappeared under it.

"This is terrible," said Robert, pressing his face up against the glass. "That's really torn it, that has."

"Don't kid yourself, Robby," said Camille. "It's not terrible at all yet, just interesting."

"It's eating up the harvest," said Robert grimly. "We'll be without bread and cattle."

"No we won't, Robby, it won't get that far."

"I hope you're right, I only hope you're right. Just look at it. The whole steppe's red with it."

"Disaster," said Camille.

All of a sudden it was twilight. A great shadow had fallen on the steppe. Robert looked over his shoulder and ran over to the east-facing window. A wide trembling cloud had covered the sun. Again Robert failed to understand what was happening. At first he was merely surprised, since there were never clouds on Rainbow during the day. But then he saw that it was birds. Thousands upon thousands of birds had flown down from the north and even through the closed windows the endless rustling of wings and the thin piercing cries were audible. Robert staggered to the table.

"Where've they come from?" he got out.

"They're saving themselves," said Camille. "They're all fleeing. I would as well if I were in your shoes, Robby. The Wave's coming."

"What Wave?" Robert bent down and looked at the instruments. "There isn't any Wave, Camille...."

"No?" said Camille coolly. "So much the better. We'll stay and see what happens."

"I wasn't going to run, either. I'm just amazed at all this. I'd better let Greenfield know anyway. And anyway where've those birds come from? There's nothing but desert up there."

"There's a lot of birds up there," said Camille. "There're great blue lakes, reeds...." He stopped.

Robert looked at him mistrustfully. In all his ten years on Rainbow he'd always believed that north of the Hot Parallel there existed neither water nor grass. No life. He thought briefly of taking the flyer and going up there with Tanya. Lakes, reeds....

The signal sounded again and Robert turned to the screen. It was Malayev himself.

"Sklyarov," said he in his usual unfriendly tone; Robert, as usual, felt guilty for everything up to and including the red rust. "Sklyarov, listen, orders. Evacuate the post at once. Bring both ulmotrons."

"Fyodor Anatolyevich," said Robert. "There's rust on the move, the birds are flying, I was just going to let you know...."

"Don't interrupt. I repeat. Get both ulmotrons and go at once by helicopter to Greenfield. Have you got that?"

"Yes."

"Now it's..." Malayev looked down. "Now it's ten forty five. You must be airborne by eleven. Bear in mind I'm sending the 'charybdis' lot out. Keep above them. If you can't manage to dismantle the ulmotrons leave them where they are."

"But what's happened?"

"The Wave's coming," said Malayev, looking Robert in the eyes for the first time. "It's passed the Hot Parallel. Hurry."

Robert stood still for a second, getting his wits together. Then he consulted the instruments again. The eruption had begun to decrease.

"Well, it's out of my hands," said Robert aloud. "Camille, give me a hand, will you?"

"I can't help anybody, now," returned Camille. "Anyway, it's not my pigeon. What shall I do—pull the ulmotrons away?"

"Yes. First we've got to disassemble them though."

"D'you want some good advice?" said Camille. "For the nth time?"

Robert had already cut off the current and, burning his fingers, was busy disconnecting the ulmotrons.

"What's the advice then?"

"Leave the ulmotrons, get into the helicopter and go to Tanya."

"Good advice, that is," said Robert, hurriedly pulling out connections. "Very pleasant. Give me a hand here to get this thing out."

The ulmotron weighed the best part of two hundredweight, a fat smooth cylinder a yard and a half long. They eased it out of its mounting and carted it to the lift. The wind began to howl and the girders were vibrating.

"That'll do," said Camille. "Let's go down together."

"We've got to get the other."

"Robby, believe me, you won't need even this one any more."

Robert consulted his watch.

"We've still got time," he said with brisk efficiency. "You go down and roll that one onto the ground."

Camille closed the lift doors and Robert returned to the

mountings. A red twilight reigned outside. There were no more birds, but across the sky hung a murky veil, through which the sun's small disk peered with difficulty. The girders were shuddering and rocking before the gusting wind.

"If only we're in time," thought Robert aloud.

Straining, he dragged out the second ulmotron, hoisted it onto his shoulder and carried it to the lift. Behind his back the window frames blew out with a shattering crash, and clouds of abrasive dust burst in, born on the baking wind. Something hit his legs with considerable force. Robert sat down hastily and propping the ulmotron against the wall, pressed the down button. The lift motor whined feebly and immediately went dead.

"Cami-i-ille!" shouted Robert, pressing his face against the grating.

There was no reply. The wind howled and whistled through the smashed windows. The signal tower was rocking so hard Robert could hardly keep his feet. He pressed the button once more. The lift didn't respond. Forcing himself forward against the wind, he made his way over to the window and looked out. The steppe was enveloped in madly swirling dust. Something flashed at the foot of the tower and Robert went cold, imagining it was the torn-off wing of a pterocar, scoured and buffeted by the gale. He shut his eyes and licked his dry lips. His mouth filled with bitterness. A beautiful trap, he thought. If Patrick were here....

"Cami-i-ille!" he shouted at the top of his voice.

He could hardly hear it himself. Through the window... no, he'd be torn to pieces. Should he move anyway? The pterocar had been smashed. What chance would he have? No, he had to get down somehow. What was Camille up to—I'd have repaired the lift if it was me... the lift!

Stepping over the wreckage, he went back to the grating and took hold of it with both hands. Now then, "Youth of the World", he thought. The door was solidly made. If the tower girders had been as good the lift would never have gone out of commission. Robert put his back against the door and with bent legs got some purchase on the walls of the lobby. One! It went dark before his eyes. Something cracked, either the door or his muscles. Once again! The door gave. It'll break down in a minute and I'll fall down the shaft. Sixty feet head over heels with the ulmotron on top of me. He turned round and put his back to the wall and his feet against the door. Cr-a-sh! The lower half of the door burst away and Robert fell on his back and hit his head on the floor. He lay for several seconds without moving. He was covered in sweat. He looked down the shaft. Away down below, he could make out the lift cabin. The thought of climbing down terrified him, but at that moment, the tower began to heel over and Robert was dragged down. He made no resistance as the tower was heeling further and further over as if it would never stop.

He climbed down, using the girders and rods as handholds, while the taut, scouring wind pressed him to the warm metal. He found time to notice that the dust was much less by now, and that the steppe was once more bathed in sunshine. The tower continued to lean over. He was in such a fury to know what had happened to the pterocar and where Camille had got to, that he jumped the last ten feet or so, jarring his legs badly and hurting his hands. The first thing he saw were Camille's fingers thrust into the dry earth.

Camille was lying beneath the overturned pterocar, his round glassy eyes open wide, and his long thin fingers were clutching at the ground as if in the attempt to drag himself clear of the wrecked machine, or perhaps his death had been hard to bear. Dust covered his white jacket and lay on his cheeks and on his open eyes.

"Camille!" called Robert.

The wind swept and tore madly at a piece of the mutilated wing above his head. It carried a stream of yellow dust along with it. It whistled and screamed in the girders of the canted tower. The tiny sun blazed furiously in the murky sky. It seemed furry somehow.

Robert got to his feet and, stumbling, tried to move the pterocar. He managed to budge the heavy machine but only for a second. He took another look at Camille. Dust covered his whole face and his jacket had become rust coloured, only the absurd white helmet remained entirely dust-free and the dull surface of the plastic gleamed cheerfully in the sunlight.

Robert's legs started to shake and he sat down next to the dead man. He felt like crying. Good-bye, Camille. I liked you, really and truly. Nobody else did but I did. I know I didn't listen to you, just as nobody else did, but I swear the only reason was that I couldn't hope to understand you. You stood head and shoulders above everyone, I wasn't within miles of you. And now I can't shift this load of earth from your poor chest. As a friend I ought to stay with you by rights. But Tanya's waiting for me, not to mention Malayev. Apart from which I very much want to live. Neither feelings nor logic will help here. I shouldn't leave you but that's just what I'm going to do. I'll run, drag myself or crawl, but I'll keep on going to the end.... I'm an idiot, I should have listened to your umpteenth bit of advice, but as usual, I didn't catch on. What was there to understand, though?...

In rising, he had to fight against his overmastering fatigue. And when he turned to take a last look at Camille, he saw the Wave.

Far away above the northern horizon, beyond the smoky

red of the settling dust, a dazzling band, brighter than the sun, shone out against the pale sky.

That's it then, thought Robert, weakly. I haven't far to go. It'll be here in half an hour and pass over, leaving a flat black desert. The tower would remain, of course, and nothing would happen to the ulmotrons, and the pterocar would still be here, and the torn-off wing would still be hanging in the hot calm. Perhaps Camille's helmet would still be here as well. There'll be nothing left of me, that's for sure. As if saying good-bye he glanced around— slapped his bare chest, felt his biceps. Pity, he thought. It was then that he noticed the flyer.

It was standing beyond the tower, a little two-seater, a bit like a gaily-coloured tortoise, fast, easy on fuel, high manoeuvrability, controls simple. It was Camille's flyer, of course, Camille's flyer!

Robert made several faltering steps towards it, then broke into a headlong gallop past the tower. He kept his eyes glued to the flyer in case it might disappear; this caused him to stumble and fall flat on his face in the prickly grass, scraping his chest and stomach in the process. He jumped to his feet and turned round. The heavy cylinder of the ulmotron, with its polished bluish sides, was still rocking from the shock of the fall. Robert looked towards the north. A black wall was already rearing up from beyond the horizon. He ran to the flyer, kicking up a cloud of dust, leapt into the seat and almost before taking hold of the wheel had the accelerator down on the floorboards.

The steppe zone stretched all the way to Greenfield and Robert covered it at an average of three hundred miles an hour. The flyer leapt over the steppe like a gigantic flea—in great hops. The dazzling band faded beyond the horizon once more. Down below everything seemed as usual—dry stubbly grass, the looming haze over the salt flats, and the rare patches of stunted scrub. The sun was blazing down without mercy. For some reason there wasn't a single trace of rust, birds or hurricane. Probably the hurricane had dispersed both of the former and had itself died out in the barren deserts of Northern Rainbow, destined by Nature herself to serve as the stage for the mad experiments of the nulls. Once, not long after Robert had arrived on Rainbow, when the Capital was still just a station and Greenfield didn't even exist, the Wave had passed over these very places as a result of the ambitious experiments of the late Liu Fin-Chen. Then everything had been burned black, but a mere seven years had passed and the tenacious, unassuming steppe grass had pushed the desert far to the north, up to the eruption regions themselves.

It'll all come back, thought Robert. It'll all be as it was. Only there'll be no Camille. And if anybody appears in the armchair behind my back, I'll know for certain it'll be a ghost. And now I'll go straight up to Malayev and tell him to his face: "I've left your ulmotrons behind." And he'll hiss through his teeth: "How dare you, Sklyarov?" Then I'll tell him: "To hell with the ulmotrons, Camille died because of your ulmotrons." And he'll say: "A great pity, of course, but you should have brought the ulmotrons." Then I'll lose my temper and come out with it all: "You're nothing but an icicle, an electronic snowman. How can you think of ulmotrons when Camille's dead?... You're heartless, you lizard!"

A hundred miles out from Greenfield, he spotted the "charybdis" force, giant telemechanical tanks surmounted with the gaping jaws of energy-absorbers. The tanks were strung out in a line from horizon to horizon, at strict half-mile intervals; from below there came the clang of metal and the roar of thousands of horsepower. On the yellow steppe behind them stretched broad bands of upturned brown earth, ploughed down to the basalt base of the continent. The caterpillar tracks flashed in the sun. Far off to the right in the darkling sky hovered a barely visible dot—the observer helicopter directing the movements of the monsters on the ground. The "charybdis" force was going out to meet the Wave.

The energy-absorbers hadn't yet come into action, apparently, but Robert was taking no chances. He climbed rapidly and only began his descent when from out of the haze ahead of him swam Greenfield—a few white houses and a square control tower, set in lush terrestrial greenery. On the northern edge of the settlement a black motionless "charybdis" squatted on a clump of crushed palm-trees, the bottomless bell of its absorber was pointing straight up at Robert. Another two of them stood to right and left of the settlement. A couple of helicopters rose from the tower and made off towards the south. The webbed wings of pterocars down in the square shone in the sun among the green lawns. People were swarming among them.

Robert took the flyer right up to the entrance of the tower and sprang out onto the wing. Someone jumped back and a woman's voice cried out: "Who's there?" Robert grabbed the handle of the glass door and froze on the instant, looking at his reflection—practically naked, caked with dust, eyes murderous, wide black scratches across chest and belly.... So what? he thought and wrenched the door open. "It's Robert," shouted somebody behind him. He went up the stairs slowly and bumped into Patrick. Patrick gazed at him open-mouthed. "Patrick, old friend, Camille's been killed." Patrick blinked and suddenly covered his mouth with his hands. Robert went on. The door to the control room was open. In there were Malayev, Shota Petrovich Pagava, the head of the northern nulls, Karl Hoffmann and one or two others, biologists probably. Robert halted in the doorway and held on to the post. There were footsteps running up the stairs behind him and somebody was shouting: "How does he know?"

"Camille..." said Robert hoarsely, he began to cough. Everyone stared at him in bewilderment.

"What's happened?" asked Malayev sharply. "What's the matter, Sklyarov, why're you in such a state?"

Robert went up to the table, and resting his grimy fists on some papers said into his face:

"Camille's dead. He was crushed."

Everything went quiet. Malayev's eyes narrowed.

"How was he crushed? Where?"

"The pterocar crushed him—all because of your precious ulmotrons. He could have got away easily but he helped me to drag out your precious ulmotrons and he got crushed. I left your ulmotrons there. Pick them up when the Wave's gone past. Do you understand? I've left them. They're lying there now."

Someone gave him a glass of water. He took it and drank greedily. Malayev said nothing. His pale face had turned quite white. Karl Hoffmann fiddled with some papers and kept his eyes down. Pagava got up and stood with his head bowed.

"It's terrible," said Malayev at last. "He was a great man." He wiped his forehead. "A very great man." He took another glance at Robert. "You're tired, Sklyarov...."

"No, I'm not."

"Get tidied up and get some rest."

"And that's all?" asked Robert bitterly.

Malayev's face was as if it had been before—hard and indifferent.

"I will detain you just a moment longer. Did you see the Wave?"

"I did. I saw the Wave as well."

"What type was it?"

Something stirred in Robert's brain, and he began to make the automatic responses. This was the powerful and intelligent director Malayev and his eternal lab assistant-observer Robert Sklyarov, the famed "Youth of the World".

"Third, I think," he said submissively. "Liu-Wave."

Pagava raised his head.

"Good!" he said with unexpected cheerfulness. At once he lost his gaiety, leaned against the table and wearily sat down. "Ah, Camille, ah, Camille," he muttered. "Poor lad!..." He took hold of his large, stick-out ears and bent his head down over his papers.

One of the biologists, with a wary glance at Robert, took Malayev by the elbow. "Excuse me but why's a Liu-Wave good?"

Malayev stopped boring into Robert with his hard eyes.

"It means," he said, "that we'll lose only the northern zone of the sowings. But we don't know it's a Liu-Wave. The observer might have made a mistake."

"Well, how's that then?" said the biologist gloomily. "We agreed, after all.... You've got these... 'charybdis'... surely you can stop it? What sort of physicists are you anyway?"

Karl Hoffmann said:

"It may be possible to extinguish the Wave's inertia on the line of the discrete overfall."

"What d'you mean—may?" exclaimed a woman standing next to the biologist. "You realize what a scandal this is? What about your guarantees? What about your pretty speeches? You realize you're leaving the planet without bread and meat?"

"I can't accept claims like that," said Malayev coldly. "I sympathize deeply, but your claims should be addressed to Etienne Lamondois. We don't run null-experiments. We study the Wave...."

Robert turned and slowly made his way to the door. Not a thought of Camille. The Wave, the harvest, meat.... Why did they dislike him so much? Because he was the cleverest of the whole lot of them? Or perhaps they didn't like anybody?

The lads were standing in the doorway, familiar faces, worried, anxious, alarmed. Somebody took his elbow. He looked up and down and finally met Patrick's sad little eyes.

"Let's go, Rob, I'll help you wash...."

"Patrick," said Robert, putting his hand on his shoulder. "Go away from here. Leave them, if you want to stay a human being."

Patrick's face twisted painfully.

"What're you talking about, Rob? Don't. All this'll pass."

"It'll pass. Nothing lasts for ever. The Wave will pass. So will life. It'll all be forgotten. Does it matter when it's forgotten? Now or later...."

The biologists were swearing out loud behind him. Malayev was demanding a summary. Pagava was shouting: "No relaxation at all! Use all the automatics! To hell with it after that!"

"Come on, Rob, let's go."

At that moment, cutting across the talking and shouting, a familiar monotonous voice thundered out in the control room:

"Attention!"

Robert turned quickly. His knees went weak. He saw on the visiplate the ugly mat helmet and the round unblinking eyes of Camille.

"I haven't got much time," Camille was saying. It was the real, living Camille. His head was shaking, his thin lips were moving and the end of his long nose twitched in time with his words. "I can't get in touch with the director. Recall the 'Arrow' at once! Evacuate the whole northern area immediately! Immediately!"

He turned his head and looked to the side, his cheek, caked with dust came into view. "Behind the Liu-Wave there's a Wave of a new type. Here's the...."

The screen flashed blindingly, and a crash was heard. The screen went dark. A grave-like silence reigned in the control room, suddenly Robert was aware of Malayev's terrible narrowed eyes fixed upon him.

4

Rainbow possessed only one spaceport, which held only one spaceship, the surface-landing D-spacer "Tariel 2". It could be seen from a considerable way off, its bluish white dome hung two hundred feet above the flat dark-green roofs of the station buildings. Gorbovsky made two uncertain circuits—it was difficult to put down near the ship itself: it was surrounded by a dense ring of vehicles of all sorts. From aloft he could see some clumsy robot fillers gripping the six tank nozzles, emergency repair robots were fussing around feeling every inch of the fuselage, as well as a robot-mother looking after a dozen brisk little analyzers. It was a normal sight, and one to gladden the eye of the tidy-minded.

Around the main hatch, however, all the rules had obviously gone over the board. The dumb spaceport cybers had been pushed to one side and their place taken by a pile of vehicles of all conceivable types. There were the usual heavy lorries, tourist buses, light "tortoises", and "leopards" and even one "mole"—this last being bulky boring machine for mining work. They were all performing odd manoeuvres near the hatch, pushing each other and squeezing each other out. To one side out in the sun, stood a number of helicopters and some empty cases which Gorbovsky identified without difficulty as the cases the ulmotrons had been packed in. There were some people sitting sadly on the cases.

Gorbovsky was beginning his third circuit still looking for a landing place when he noticed a heavy pterocar right behind him, the pilot of which was hanging half way out of his door and signalling to him unintelligibly. Gorbovsky set the flyer down between the helicopters and the packing cases and the pterocar at once made a clumsy landing beside him.

"I'm after you," shouted the pilot crisply, leaping out of his cockpit.

"I wouldn't if I were you," said Gorbovsky softly. "I've got nothing to do with the queue. I'm the captain of this spaceship."

The pilot's face expressed admiration.

"Wonderful!" he exclaimed in a low voice, taking a careful look around.

"Now we'll show those nulls what's what.... What do they call the captain of the ship?"

"Gorbovsky," said Gorbovsky with a slight bow.

"Navigator?"

"Falkenstein."

"Lovely," said the pilot crisply. "So you're Gorbovsky, I'm Falkenstein. Let's go."

He took Gorbovsky by the elbow. The latter resisted.

"Listen, Gorbovsky, there's no risk attached. I know my way about these ships. I came here on one. We'll get through to the stores, grab an ulmotron each and shut ourselves in the ward-room. When it's all over," he gave a negligent wave at the crowd of vehicles, "we'll get away on the quiet."

"What if the real navigator turns up?"

"He'll have a hard job proving that he is the real navigator," returned the usurper weightily.

Gorbovsky giggled:

"Okay, let's go."

The fake navigator smoothed his hair, took a deep breath and strode forward resolutely. They began squeezing through the machines. The fake navigator talked without stopping. He had suddenly developed a deep, impressive bass voice.

"I suppose," he announced for general consumption,

"that cleaning the diffusers would only hold us up. I suggest we simply replace half the sets and pay special attention to the fuselage ... move your car a bit there, mate! You're in the way. So, Valentin Petrovich, when we come out onto deritrinitation ... back your lorry up, mate. I don't see why all this crush. There's a queue, you know, a list of who's who ... one of you go up at a time. I don't know about you, Valentin Petrovich, but I'm amazed at the manners of the natives. We never saw the like even on Pandora with the Tahorgs...."

"You're absolutely right, Mark," said Gorbovsky, enjoying himself.

"What? Yes, naturally ... terrible manners."

A girl wearing a silk headscarf stuck her head out of the cabin of a heavy lorry and inquired:

"Navigator and captain, I presume?"

"Yes!" said the navigator, a challenge in his voice. "And as navigator I recommend you to read the unloading schedule again."

"You think I should?"

"Absolutely. You shouldn't have brought your lorry into the twenty-yard zone."

"You know, men," a cheerful voice rang out, "this navigator's got less imagination than the first two."

"And what exactly is that supposed to mean?" asked the fake navigator, much offended. His face had something of the false Nero about it.

"You realize," went on the girl in the headscarf, piercingly, "that over there on the empty cases, there are already two navigators and one captain. The empty cases had ulmotrons in them once. The ship's engineer got away with them—nice quiet young woman too. The Council's representative's after her just now...."

"How d'you like that, Valentin Petrovich?" cried the fake. "Impostors, eh?"

"I have the feeling," said Gorbovsky thoughtfully, "that I'm not going to get aboard my own ship."

"Too right," said the girl in the headscarf. "Not original, either."

The navigator was all for pushing on, but the lorry on the right turned in slightly, while a black and yellow bus standing on the left edged a touch to the right, and the way ahead to the beckoning hatch was cut off by the "mole" growling and baring its teeth, and throwing up the odd clump of earth.

"Valentin Petrovich!" exclaimed the fake indignantly. "I can't answer for the ship in such circumstances!"

"Old hat!" remarked the driver of the bus gloomily.

A cheerful voice rang out:

"This isn't much fun! Bores you stiff, he does. Remember the second navigator—he was a boy! Remember how he pulled his shirt off to show where he'd been hit by meteors!"

"No, the first one was better," said the driver of the "mole", turning round.

"Yes he was good," agreed the girl in the headscarf.

The fake navigator, crushed, fell to picking clods of earth from the shining teeth of the "mole".

"Well, and what have you got to say for yourself?" the driver of the bus addressed himself to Gorbovsky. "What are you keeping quiet for? You have to say something. Something convincing."

Everybody waited with curiosity.

"Of course I could get in through the passenger door," said Gorbovsky, after some thought.

The fake navigator lifted his head and looked at him hopefully.

"No you couldn't," the driver shook his head. "They're locked from inside."

62

In the ensuing pause Kaneko's voice could be heard distinctly:

"I can't give you ten, you understand, Comrade Prozorovsky?"

"And you understand me, Comrade Kaneko! We've an order in for ten. How can I go back with only six?"

Somebody joined in:

"Take them, Prozorovsky, take six for now. Four of ours will be free in a week, I'll send them over."

"Is that a promise?"

The girl in the headscarf was speaking:

"I feel really sorry for Prozorovsky. They've got sixteen projects on ulmotrons!"

"Yes, they're hard up," sighed the driver of the bus.

"We've got five," said the fake navigator sadly. "Five projects and only one ulmotron. You'd think it'd be worth their while to fetch two hundred."

"We could have brought two hundred or three hundred," said Gorbovsky, "but everybody wants ulmotrons now. They've laid down six new U-conveyers on Earth."

"U-conveyer!" said the girl in the headscarf. "Have you any idea of the what goes into an ulmotron?"

"A general idea."

"A hundredweight of ultramicroelements... hand assembly, half-micron tolerances.... What self-respecting person would work as an assembler? Would you?"

"They get volunteers," said Gorbovsky.

"Ah!" remarked the driver of the "mole", obviously repelled. "Help the Physicists' Week!..."

"Well, then, Valentin Petrovich," said the navigator, with a rueful smile. "It seems they won't let us through."

"Call me Leonid Andreyevich."

"And me Hans," confessed the fake navigator in a depressed tone. "Let's go over and sit on the cases. Something might turn up."

The girl in the headscarf waved them good-bye. They made their way out between the piles of vehicles and sat down on the cases next to the other fake spacemen. They were greeted by a silence compounded equally of sympathy and scorn.

Gorbovsky fingered the case. The plastic was rough and hard. It was hot out in the sun. Gorbovsky hadn't the slightest reason for being here, but, as always, he had a driving urge to get to know these men, find out what had brought them here and how they were getting on in general. He put several boxes together and after asking "May I?" lay down at full length and clamped the micro-conditioner near his head. Then he switched on his recorder.

"They call me Gorbovsky," he said by way of introduction. "Leonid. I was the captain of this spaceship."

"So was I," informed a thickset dark-faced man sitting on Gorbovsky's right. "My name's Alpa."

"I'm Banin," announced a lean youth. Though naked to the waist, he was wearing a white panama. "I was the navigator and still am. At any rate till I get an ulmotron."

"Hans," said the fake Falkenstein shortly, settling himself on the grass close to the conditioner.

The third false navigator apparently had not heard them. He sat with his back to them and went on writing something on a pad balanced on his knees.

A long-nosed "leopard" emerged from the crowd. The doors opened for empty ulmotron boxes to fly out and then the machine accelerated on into the steppe.

"Prozorovsky," said Banin with envy.

"Yes," said Alpa bitterly. "He doesn't need to lie. Lamondois' right hand." He sighed deeply. "Never did I lie. I can't stand lying. Now I've got a bad conscience about it."

Banin said profoundly:

"If a man is forced to lie against all his inclination, it means there's something wrong somewhere."

"It's the system that's wrong," said Hans. "It all stems from the premise: the one who gets results gets the ulmotrons."

"And you want a different system," said Gorbovsky. "No results, there's your ulmotron. You get results, go and sit on the boxes."

"Yes," said Alpa. "It's this terrible frustration. Who ever heard of queues for equipment? Or energy? You gave them your indent and you got your supplies. You never even gave a thought to where they got it from. That is, you realized subconsciously that there was a mass of people working in the field of science supply—and liking it. Incidentally it really is interesting work. I remember after school I used to work myself assembling better neutron hook-ups—and enjoyed it. Nobody remembers it now, but it was a very popular method at one time—neutron analysis."

He drew from his pocket a blackened pipe and filled it with unhurried and confident movements. Everyone watched him with curiosity.

"We all know that the ratio of users and makers has not changed since then. But a sort of fantastic leap in demand has taken place. Judging by what I see around me, the average research worker nowadays needs twenty times as much energy and equipment as in my day." He inhaled deeply, his pipe gurgled. "It's understandable enough. It's always been reckoned that the problem that sparks off most new ideas gets the most attention. It's natural, you can't have it any other way. But if the initial problem lies on the subelectronic level and demands, let's say, a single unit of equipment, every one of the problems it gives rise to takes things a stage lower at least and demands tens of units. And that's not mentioning the fact that the interests of the producers don't always coincide with those of the consumers."

"It's a vicious circle," said Banin. "The economists have boobed."

"The economists are research scientists as well," objected Alpa. "They've got loads of problems to deal with too. And now we've started talking about it, here's a curious paradox, I've noticed recently. Take null-T now, a new problem full of possibilities and prospects of development. As it's got plenty of possibilities, Lamondois quite properly gets enormous allotments of plant and energy. To keep this Lamondois is forced to drive ahead—faster, deeper and...narrower. And the faster and deeper he penetrates the more he needs, and the less he has till he puts the brake on himself. Take a look at that queue. Forty people are standing about and wasting valuable time. A full third of all the research workers on Rainbow are wasting their time—not to speak of nervous energy and concentration. The other two-thirds are sitting about their labs twiddling their thumbs and thinking of one thing and one thing only: Will they bring one or not? Isn't this really self-braking? The urge to keep the stream of supplies flowing starts a race, the race gives rise to a disproportionate growth in the number of demands on those supplies, and self-restraint comes about as a result."

Alpa stopped speaking and began knocking out his pipe. The "mole" burst out from the crowd of vehicles shoving them right and left. The cap of a new ulmotron could be seen sticking up by the window of the absurdly high cabin. As he went by the driver waved at the pseudo-spacers.

"I'd like to know what the Pathfinders want an ulmotron for," muttered Hans.

Nobody answered. Everybody was watching the retreating "mole", and the back board adorned with the identification mark of the Pathfinder corps—a black heptagon on a red shield.

"All the same," said Banin, "it's the economists' fault. They should have foreseen it. They should have set up schools twenty years ago and we'd have had a decent number of supply workers now."

"I don't know," said Alpa. "Can you plan a thing like that? Of course, we don't know that much about it but it might be that you simply can't balance the spiritual potential of the research workers and their material needs. To put it crudely, there'll always be lots more ideas than ulmotrons."

"Well, that's still got to be proved," said Banin.

"Well, I never said it had been proved, did I? I was only supposing."

"A grim supposition, don't you think?" Banin announced. He was beginning to get belligerent. "You're suggesting an eternal crisis! It's a dead end!"

"Why a dead end?" asked Gorbovsky quietly. "Just the opposite."

Banin wasn't listening.

"We've got to find a way out of the crisis," he was saying. "We've got to look for a way out. And we won't find it in gloomy suggestions!"

"Really, why're they so gloomy?" said Gorbovsky. But still nobody paid any attention to him.

"You've got to stick to the basic principle of distribution," went on Banin. "That would simply be unfair to our best workers. You spend twenty years chewing over one little problem and they give you as much energy as Lamondois gets, eh? It's ridiculous! That means the answer isn't here. Not here. Do you see the way out yourselves? Or are you sticking to registration?"

"I'm an old scientist and an old man," said Alpa. "All my life I've been a physicist. I know I haven't done all

5*

that much, but that doesn't matter, I'm just a run of the mill research worker. In spite of all these new theories, I'm still convinced that scientific knowledge is the purpose of human life. And to tell the truth, it sickens me to see thousands of people these days steering clear of science and finding their vocation in a sentimental relationship with nature, art they call it. They are content to skim over the surface of things, calling that aesthetic appreciation. To my way of thinking history herself has divided mankind into three groups: soldiers of science, educators and doctors, incidentally, they're soldiers of science as well. Science is just getting over the period of material shortage and yet you find thousands of people drawing pictures, rhyming words ... composing impressions. There's a lot of potential workers among them too. Energy, intelligence and fantastic application."

"Well, well!" said Banin.

Alpa said nothing and began filling his pipe.

"Let me take your argument a bit further if I may," said Gorbovsky. "I see you haven't the courage."

"Have a try then."

"All these artists and writers want putting in special camps, their pens and brushes should be taken away and they should be put through a short course and set to turning out new U-conveyers, tau-tractors and ertochronic prisms for the soldiers of science...."

"Rubbish!" said the disappointed Banin.

"Yes, it's rubbish," agreed Alpa. "But our ideas don't depend on our likes and dislikes. That idea is deeply repugnant to me, it even frightens me, but it's been mentioned and not only by me."

"It'll never lead to anything," said Gorbovsky lazily gazing up into the sky. "It's an attempt to iron out the contradiction between the general spiritual and material potential of mankind as a whole. It leads to a new contradiction, a stale one at that—between machine logic and the system of morals and education. When they clash machine logic always comes off worst."

Alpa nodded, wrapped in clouds of smoke. Hans went on thoughtfully:

"It's a terrible idea. Remember the 'Ten-man Project'? When it was suggested to the Council that part of the abundance reserve should be fed into the science grids?... To starve mankind a bit in the cause of pure science. Remember the slogan, 'Scientists are ready to starve'?"

Banin added:

"And Yamakawa stood up as well and said: 'But six million children aren't. Just as you aren't ready to work on the social planning side.' "

"I don't like fanatics either," said Gorbovsky.

"Not long ago I was reading a book by Lorentz," said Hans. "**People and Problems** ... know it?"

"Yes," said Gorbovsky.

Alpa shook his head.

"Fine book, isn't it? There was one idea there that shook me. Lorentz doesn't dwell on it, mind, mentions it in passing."

"Well?" said Banin.

"I thought it over the whole of one night, I remember. We didn't have enough gear and we were waiting till some more was delivered—you know how nerve-racking it gets. So I came to this conclusion. Lorentz talks about natural selection operating in science. Which factors determine the direction of science these days when science has very little bearing on man's material well-being?"

"Well?" said Banin.

"So I came to the following conclusion. After a while those scientific researches that are the most successful will gather all the supplies to themselves and the rest will just fizzle out. And all research will consist of two or

69

three directions and only the top men will have any idea of what they're doing. See what I mean?"

"Tripe," said Banin.

"Why is it tripe?" asked Hans, offended. "Look at the facts. There are hundreds of thousands of possible lines of research. Thousands of people work in each one of them. I personally know four groups who have packed up because they weren't getting anywhere and joined other groups who were. I've done it twice myself."

Alpa said:

"All joking aside, take Lamondois. He's breaking his neck to get null-T going. Null-T will lead to a load of new lines of inquiry, that's only to be expected. But Lamondois is forced to chop off all these branches, he's forced to simply ignore them. Because he can't study every branch carefully and follow it as far as it will go. What's more he's forced to ignore consciously things which are well known to be interesting, fascinating. That's what happened with the Wave, for example. Unexpected, astonishing, and to my mind, dangerous. But Lamondois has gone as far as to provoke a split in the camp, because he's so set on his own aim. He's quarrelled with Aristotle, and he's refusing to guarantee supplies to the Wave-men. He's going deeper, deeper, deeper, and his problem's getting narrower and narrower. The Wave's left far behind and forgotten. It's only a hindrance to him, he doesn't want to hear about it. While it's burning the wheatfields, by the way."

The loudspeaker roared out over the spaceport.

"Attention, Rainbow! Director speaking. Senior test man Gaba and his crew to report to me at once."

"Lucky so-and-sos," said Hans. "They've got no ulmotrons to worry about."

"They've got enough worries of their own," said Banin. "I watched them training once—no thanks I'd sooner be

70

a fake navigator. Then to sit for two years doing nothing and hear every day: 'Bear up a little bit longer. Tomorrow maybe.' "

"I'm glad you mentioned the 'rear' of science," said Gorbovsky, "the blank spots. I'm interested in that too. To my mind things aren't good back there. The Massachusetts machine for instance." Here Alpa nodded. Gorbovsky addressed him. "You remember it, of course. Now it's almost forgotten. Cybernetics has had its day."

"I don't remember anything about any Massachusetts machine," said Banin. "Well?"

"You know the old fear. Machines would become cleverer than men and take them over. About fifty years ago in Massachusetts they made the most complicated cyber mechanism the world had ever seen. It had phenomenal speed and a fantastic memory and so forth. It worked exactly four minutes. They switched it off, cemented up all the ways in and out, cut off the energy supply, mined it and put barbed wire round it. Ordinary rusty barbed wire, don't believe me if you don't want to."

"What exactly was the matter?" asked Banin.

"It had started to run itself," said Gorbovsky.

"I don't get it."

"Nor do I, but they only just managed to switch it off."

"Does anybody understand it?"

" 'I've talked to one of the men who made it. He took me by the shoulder and looked me straight in the eye and said only: 'Leonid, it was terrible.' "

"Terrific," said Hans.

"Ah, tripe," said Banin. "That sort of thing just doesn't nterest me."

"Well it does me," said Gorbovsky. "Somebody might switch it on again, you know. The Council have forbidden it, of course, but the ban could be lifted."

Alpa growled:

"Every age has its own wizards and ghosts."

"Incidentally, a propos," put in Gorbovsky. "I always remember the case of the 'Baker's Dozen'."

Hans' eyes lit up.

"The case of the 'Baker's Dozen'—now that's really something!" said Banin. "Thirteen fanatics.... By the way where are they now?"

"Wait a minute, wait a minute," said Alpa. "Are those the scientists that connected themselves to machines? But didn't they die?"

"So they say, yes," said Gorbovsky, "but that's not the point. The precedent was set."

"Well, what of it?" asked Banin. "They call them fanatics but there's something attractive about them all the same. To be rid of all these weaknesses and passions, emotional outbursts.... The naked intellect plus unlimited possibilities for the perfecting of the organism. A researcher who doesn't need instruments, who is his own instrument and transport. No queues for ulmotrons either.... I can see it all. The flyer-man, the reactor-man, the laboratory-man. Invulnerable, immortal...."

"I'm sorry," Alpa growled, "but they won't be men, they'll be Massachusetts machines."

"How did they die if they're supposed to be immortal?" asked Hans.

"They destroyed themselves," said Gorbovsky. "Apparently it's not so hot being a laboratory-man after all."

A man purple from exertion appeared from behind the vehicles with an ulmotron across his shoulders. Banin jumped down from his box and ran to give him a hand. Gorbovsky watched thoughtfully as between them they loaded the ulmotron into the helicopter. The purple man was complaining:

"It's not that they give you one instead of three. It's not that you lose half a day waiting for it. You've got

72

to prove you've got a right to have it! They don't believe you! Can you imagine that—they don't believe you! Don't believe you!!!"

When Banin got back, Alpa said:

"It's all rather amazing, isn't it? If you're interested in the rear regions of science take a careful look at the Wave. Every week there's the usual null-transmission. Every transmission sets up a Wave. There's an eruption, large or small. But they only take an amateur interest in the Wave. That way will get a Massachusetts machine— only this time we won't be able to stop it. Camille—you know Camille?—looks on it as a planetary phenomenon, but nobody can understand what he says. He's a hard chap to work with."

"Incidentally," said Hans, "do you know what Camille thinks about the future? He reckons that the current interest in science is a sort of gratitude for the abundance it's brought, a hangover from the time when the capacity for logical thought was the only hope of mankind. He says: 'Humanity is on the brink of a split. The emotionalists and the logicals—I think he means artistic people and scientists—are drifting poles apart, are ceasing to understand each other and ceasing to need each other. Man is born either an emotionalist or a logical. It's in his very nature. And sometime the human race is going to split into two societies, and they'll be just as alien to each other as we are to the Leonids.' "

"Well, that's a load of rubbish," said Banin. "What do you mean split? Where does your average man go to then? Pagava might look at one of Surd's pictures like a sheep looks at a new gate, and Surd might not even know that Pagava exists, that I grant you—you've got your logical and emotionalist. But what about me? I'm a research worker, yes. Three-quarters of my time and nerves are devoted to science. But I can't do without art either! I can hear

73

somebody's recorder on here and I like it. I could get on without it but I prefer to hear it...so where's your split?"

"I thought that too," said Hans. "But he said that the genius of our society would be the average man of the future; then he said that there are two sorts of average man—the emotionalist and the logical. Anyway, that's how I understood him."

"I'm lost in admiration," said Banin. "As far as I'm concerned, when Camille talks you can't understand a word."

"Maybe it was one of Camille's usual paradoxes?" said Gorbovsky deep in thought. "He loves paradoxes. Though it's a bit straightforward for a paradox, I will say."

"Well, Leonid Andreyevich, you've got to remember it's not Camille's ideas, it's mine," said Hans. "I was sunbathing on the beach yesterday when Camille appeared suddenly on a rock—you know the way he has?—and started thinking aloud, talking mainly to the waves. I lay and listened, then I fell asleep."

Everybody laughed.

"Camille's setting himself problems," said Gorbovsky. "I can imagine more or less why he needs that split. He's working on the evolution of humanity apparently and he's constructing models. A synthesis of emotionalists and logicals seems to him like a new sort of man, one who won't be a man any longer."

Alpa sighed and put his pipe away.

"Problems, problems," said he. "Contradictions, synthesis, rear, front.... You'll have noticed who're sitting here? You, you, him, me. Failures, the scrap, heap of science. There are the scientists over there getting the ulmotrons."

He would have said something more, but the loudspeaker cut across his words:

"Attention, Rainbow! Director speaking. Captain of spaceship 'Tariel 2', Leonid Andreyevich Gorbovsky. Energy planner Kaneko. Please report to me at once."

At once drivers stuck their heads out of their cabins. Pure pleasure was written across their faces. They were all looking at the fake spacemen. Banin hunched himself up and spread his hands. Hans called out gaily: "It's not me, I'm the navigator!" Alpa groaned and covered his face with his hands. Gorbovsky got up hurriedly.

"Time for me to go," he said. "I certainly don't want to. I didn't have a chance to finish what I was saying, either. My view's this, cutting it short. You needn't get all sad and start wringing your hands. Life is marvellous. Because, incidentally, of all the contradictions and new ways of looking at things. As far as unavoidable suffering is concerned, I love Kuprin, and he's got a hero somewhere, a man who's a drunk and in a complete mess. I can remember his words off by heart." He cleaned his throat. "If I fall under a train, and my stomach gets ripped open and my insides get mixed with sand and spread all over the wheels, and if they ask me in that last moment: 'Well, is life marvellous now?' I'll say, with grateful ecstasy, 'Ah, how marvellous it is!'" Gorbovsky gave an embarrassed smile and crammed his recorder into his pocket. "That was written three centuries ago, when humanity was still on all fours. Let's stop complaining! I'll leave you the conditioner—it's mighty hot out here."

5

Matvei was not alone. A small dark-haired man with dark eyes was sitting on his table. His hands were tucked beneath him and he was swinging his legs. He looked a bit like a school-leaver. It was Etienne Lamondois, the leader of contemporary null-physics, "fast physics" man, as his colleagues called him.

"May I come in?" asked Gorbovsky.

"And here he is," said Matvei. "You know each other?"

Lamondois leaped quickly from the table, came up close to Gorbovsky and wrung his hand firmly, looking him up and down as he did so.

"Glad to see you, captain," he said with a pleasant smile. "We were just talking about you."

Gorbovsky stepped back and sat down in an armchair.

"And we about you," he said.

Etienne bowed in lively fashion and returned to his table near the director.

"So, let me go on. The 'charybdis' lot are fighting it out to the last. We've got to give Malayev his due: those are marvellous machines. It's funny the northern Wave being of a quite new type. The lads have given it a name already—you know what? They've called it P-Wave after Shota. Hell's bells I've got to own up, I'm tearing my hair out. Why didn't I pay attention to this marvellous phenomenon before this? I'll have to apologize to Aristotle. He's right after all. He and Camille. I take my hat off to Camille. I've done that before but now I think I understand what he was driving at. Incidentally, you know he was killed?"

Matvei twitched his head.

"Again?"

"Oh, you know already! It's a queer story. He died

76

and came alive again. I've heard of such things. There's nothing new under the sun. Jesus Christ did it after all. By the way, can you believe that Sklyarov would have left him to be overrun by the Wave? I can't for one. So the northern Wave has reached the belt of observation posts. The first Wave—the Liu-Wave has dispersed. The second one, the P-Wave is driving back the 'charybdis' tanks at the rate of 15 miles an hour. So the northern sown areas have had it, anyway. We'll have to send the biologists by helicopters. . . ."

"I know," said the director. "They've been complaining."

"What do they expect? I can understand how they feel but I can't help thinking they've behaved with less dignity than I should have expected. The advance of the Wave on the sea has been checked. Liu would have given half his life to see what's going on there: nothing less than the deformation of the ring Wave. This dislocation is in line with the Kappa equation, and if the Wave is a Kappa field, then everything poor Malayev has been racking his brains over is clear: D-penetration, telegenous nature of the fountains, and the 'secondary manifestation'. . . . Hell's bells in the last three hours we've learned more about the Wave than we've done in the last ten years! Matvei, bear in mind, as soon as this lot is over, we'll need a U-registrator, maybe two. Right I've put in my indent, okay? An ordinary computer won't be up to it. It's only Liu-algorithms, Liu-logic."

"Okay, okay," said Matvei. "What about the south?"

"The south's alright, it's all ocean. The Wave got as far as Pushkin shore, burned up the Southern Archipelago and stopped. I get the impression that it'll go no further, and it's a pity because the observers cleared out of there so fast that they left all the automatic equipment behind so we know next to nothing about the southern Wave."

77

He clicked his fingers in annoyance. "I know that isn't your concern, but what's to be done, Matvei? Let's look at things realistically. Rainbow's a physicists' planet. It's our laboratory. Energy stations have been destroyed and can't be put back. When this experiment is finished we'll build them again together. We'll want tons of energy, you know! And as far as the fisheries are concerned, well, Hell's bells.... Nulls are willing to do without squid soup! Don't be angry with us, Matvei."

"I'm not angry," said the director, with a heavy sigh. "But there's something childish about you all the same, Etienne. Like a child, you break in play things that adults care a lot about." He sighed again. "Try to preserve the southern grain areas at all events. I'd hate to lose our autonomy here."

Lamondois glanced at his watch and darted out without a word. The director regarded Gorbovsky.

"How do you like that, Leonid?" he asked, with a humourless smile. "Yes, my friend. Poor Postysheva! She's an angel compared to these vandals. When I think that in addition to all my worries I've got to muck about setting up a new supply and night worker system my hair stands on end." He pulled at his moustache. "But on the other hand Lamondois' right—Rainbow is a physicists' planet. But what'll Kaneko say or Gina... ." He shook his head and shuddered. "Yes, Kaneko! Where's Kaneko?"

"Matvei," said Gorbovsky, "may I know why you sent for me?"

The director, who now had his back to him and was fiddling with the keys of the selector asked:

"Are you comfortable there?"

"Yes," said Gorbovsky. He was already reclining.

"Feel like a drink?"

"Okay."

"Get one from the refrigerator. Want anything to eat?"

"Not yet but I will."

"We'll have a talk then. Now don't stop me working."

Gorbovsky got the drinks out of the frig and mixed himself a cocktail lying back in the chair. It was soft and cool, the cocktail delicious and icy. He lay with his eyes half closed in pleasure, sipping from his glass and listening to the director talking to Kaneko. Kaneko was saying that he couldn't get out—they wouldn't let him go. The director was asking: "Who won't let you go?" "There's forty men here and none of them will let me go," answered Kaneko. "I'll send Gaba over right away," said the director. Kaneko objected to the effect that it was noisy enough over there already. Then Matvei told him about the Wave and reminded him in an apologetic tone that he, Kaneko, was the chief of the SIS on Rainbow. Kaneko said angrily that he didn't remember any such thing, and Gorbovsky felt for him.

Men in charge of the Service for Individual Security always attracted feelings of sympathy and pity. There appeared on every planet, sooner or later, whatever its state of development, outsiders—tourists, holiday-makers (children and all), free artists looking for new ideas, failures looking for solitude or heavy work, sundry dilettantes, hunters and the like, none of them on any list, none of them known on the planet, with no ties locally— indeed avoiding such ties strenuously. The chief of the SIS was obliged to make the acquaintance of every outsider, to instruct them and make sure that each one of them signalled his whereabouts to the Central Registry. On hostile planets like Yaila and Pandora where the newcomer was dogged by danger at every step SIS teams had saved more than one life. On a planet like Rainbow, flat as a pancake, with its equable climate, shortage of animal life and its ever-calm sea, the SIS was bound to lapse and the signs were that it had turned into an empty formality. Polite, meticulous Kaneko, feeling the ambiguous nature of his position, had been busy, of course, with his planning or other real work, and not with instructing writers who had come in search of solitude, or following the intended routes of lovers and honey-mooners.

"How many outsiders are there on Rainbow at present?" asked Matvei.

"About sixty. Maybe a few more."

"Kaneko, old friend, all outsiders have got to be rounded up at once and sent off to the Capital."

"I don't quite understand the meaning of this measure," said Kaneko politely. "Outsiders are very rare in the threatened areas. There's just dry barren steppe there, it smells bad and it's very hot. . . ."

"Don't let's argue, please, Kaneko," pleaded Matvei. "The Wave is the Wave. At times like this it's better for all uncommitted personnel to be where we can keep an eye on them. Gaba'll be here soon with his layabouts and I'll send him over. Sort it out there."

Gorbovsky put his straw aside and drank straight from the glass. Camille died, he thought. Died and rose from the dead. I've known such things too. Their famous Wave's causing quite a panic by the looks of things. During a panic some people always die and you're astonished to see them in a café a million miles from where it happened. His face is scratched, his voice a bit hoarse but strong, he listens to the tales being swapped and helps himself to a portion of marinaded shrimps with Setzuan cabbage.

"Matvei," he called. "Where's Camille at the moment?"

"Oh, yes, you don't know yet," said the director. He went over to the table and started to mix himself a cocktail out of pomegranate and pineapple juice. "Malayev was talking to me from Greenfield. Camille somehow turned up at the forward post and was held up there and overrun by the Wave. The story's a bit mixed up. This

Sklyarov—he's an observer—came whizzing in on Camille's flyer, threw a fit of hysterics, and said that Camille had been crushed to death, and within ten minutes Camille appears on the screen at Greenfield, gives out a prophecy as usual and disappears. It's hard to take Camille seriously after a trick like that."

"He's a card alright. Who's Sklyarov?"

"One of Malayev's observers, I'm telling you. He tries hard and he's a nice boy, no genius mind. . . . To think he would abandon Camille is absolutely out of the question. Malayev's always getting these crazy ideas."

"Don't blame Malayev," said Gorbovsky. "He's only being logical. Anyway, let's not talk about that. What about the Wave?"

"Okay," said the director vaguely.

"Is it very dangerous?"

"What?"

"The Wave, is it dangerous?"

Matvei let out a breath.

"The Wave, generally speaking, is deadly dangerous," he said. "The trouble is that the physicists never know in advance how it's going to behave. It can disperse at any moment." He was silent. "Or it may not."

"No protection from it?"

"I never heard of anybody trying. They say it's an awful sight."

"Surely you've seen it?"

Matvei's moustaches began to bristle menacingly.

"You may have noticed," he said, "that I haven't got much time for tearing about the planet. I'm the whole time waiting for somebody, or pacifying people, or somebody's waiting for me. . . . I tell you if I had any spare time. . . ."

"Matvei, I expect you wanted my help in looking for outsiders," inquired Gorbovsky cautiously.

The director glanced at him angrily.

"Hungry yet?"

"N-no."

Matvei prowled round his study.

"Well, I'll tell you what's bothering me. First of all Camille said this experiment would end badly. They paid no attention to that. Nor did I. Now Lamondois confesses Camille was right. . . ."

The door swung open and with a flash of wonderful teeth a huge young Negro burst into the room. He was wearing brief white shorts, a white jacket and white shoes on his bare feet.

"I've arrived!" he announced with a sweep of his enormous arms. "What is your wish my lord director? You wish me to lay the town in ruins or to build you a palace? Guessing your desires I wished to carry off for you the most beautiful of women, by name Gina Pickbridge, her spells, however, proved the stronger and she remains at the Fisheries and sends you her unflattering greetings."

"What have I got to do with it?" asked the director. "Let her send her greetings to Lamondois."

"Truly, let her!" exclaimed the Negro.

"Gaba, you know about the Wave?"

"Call that a Wave?" said the Negro scornfully. "When I get into that capsule and Lamondois presses the lever, that'll be a Wave! This one—why it's nothing, a ripple! But I hear you and am ready to obey."

"Have you got the brigade with you?" asked the director patiently. Gaba indicated the window silently. "Nip along with them to the spaceport and do what Kaneko tells you."

"Our heads and eyes are his," said Gaba. At that moment several lusty throats roared out to a guitar the tune of the old psalm **The Walls of Jericho**:

On happy Rainbow,
On   Rainbow,   Rainbow...

Gaba was at the window in one stride. "Quiet!" he barked.

The song died away. A thin clear voice wailed a lament:

> Dig my grave both long and narrow,
> Make my coffin neat and strong!

"I go," said Gaba, not without embarrassment. A powerful leap took him over the windowsill.

"Children," muttered the director, grinning. He let the window down. "The lads are getting restive. I don't know what I'd do without them."

He stayed by the window and Gorbovsky studied his back with half-closed eyes. It was broad enough but there was something hunched and unhappy about it, so much so that Gorbovsky began to feel uneasy. A back like that didn't belong to a spaceman and explorer like Matvei.

"Matvei," said Gorbovsky. "Do you really need me?"

"Yes," said the director. "Really." He continued to stare out of the window.

"Matvei, tell me what's the matter."

"Angst, foreboding, worry," Matvei declaimed and stopped.

Gorbovsky squirmed himself comfortable and quietly switched on his recorder. Just as quietly he remarked:

"Okay, old friend. I'll just sit here with you."

"That's it, just you sit there."

A guitar twanged sad and lazy, beyond the window burned the empty sky, while in the study reigned a cool gloom.

"Wait, we'll wait," said the director loudly and returned to his chair. Gorbovsky said nothing.

"Of all the things!" he exclaimed. "Aren't I rude! I'd clean forgot. How's Zhenya?"

"Well, thanks."

"She hasn't come back?"

"No, she hasn't come back. She doesn't even want to think about that now, if you ask me."

"Still Alyosha?"

"Naturally. It's fantastic how important that's turned out to be for her."

"Remember how she swore: 'Just let it be borne!' "

"I remember. I can remember what you can't. She had an awful time with him at first. Used to complain. 'I've got no maternal feelings, I'm a freak, I'm made of stone.' Then something happened; I didn't even notice how it came about. He's a fine lad, mind. He's got sweet ways, clever as well. I was walking once with him in the park. Suddenly he asks: 'Dad, who's that sitting down over there?' At first I didn't understand. Then . . . you know how the wind rocks the lamp, well it was casting its shadow on the wall. 'Sitting down,' it's a good description, isn't it?"

"Yes," said Gorbovsky. "He'll be a writer one day. It'd still be a good idea to send him to boarding school."

Matvei waved his hand.

"No good wasting breath," he said. "She won't give him up. As you know I argued at first, then I thought: 'Why? Why take from a person the reason for living?' That's what she lives for. I don't understand it," he confessed, "but I can see it in her. Perhaps it's because I'm so much older than her. And Alyosha came on the scene too late for me. I sometimes wonder how lonely I'd be if I didn't know I could see him every day. Zhenya says I love him more like a grandfather than a father. Well she may be right. Can you understand what I'm talking about?"

"I understand. But it's strange to me. I was never lonely."

"Yes," said Matvei. "For as long as I've known you, you've always been in the centre of a crowd. And they all need you. You've a fine character, everyone likes you."

"That's not it," said Gorbovsky. "I like everybody, that's it. I've lived the best part of a hundred years, think of it, Matvei, and I've never yet met an unpleasant individual."

"You're a very rich man," said Matvei.

"Incidentally," recalled Gorbovsky, "there's a book come out in Moscow, **Thy Bitter Joy**—it's by Sergei Volkovoi. The latest thing from the emotionalists. Genkin came out with a bilious article. Very witty but not very convincing. Literature, so he said, should be pleasant to 'dissect'. The emotionalists had a nasty laugh at that one. The row's probably going on now. I'll never understand it. Why can't they tolerate one another?"

"It's very simple," said Matvei. "Each one of them thinks he's making history."

"But he is! Everyone of them really is making history! We, the scientists and engineers, are under their influence whether we like it or not."

"I don't feel like arguing about it," said Matvei. "I've got no time to think about it, Leonid. I'm not under their influence anyway."

"Well, don't let's argue then. Let's drink this stuff instead. If you like I'll even drink your wine. But only if it'll do you some good."

"There's only one thing that'll do me any good at the moment and that's for Lamondois to turn up here disappointed and say the Wave's fizzled out."

For a while they drank in silence regarding each other over their glasses.

"Nobody's rung you up for ages," said Gorbovsky. "It's odd rather."

"It's the Wave. Everybody's busy. They've forgotten to fight each other—they've all bolted off somewhere."

The door of the study opened and Etienne Lamondois appeared on the threshold. His face was thoughtful and his movements were unusually slow and measured. The director and Gorbovsky watched him come in in silence and Gorbovsky felt an unpleasant sensation in the pit of his stomach. He had as yet no idea of what was happening or had happened, but he knew already that the time for lying comfortably in his armchair was over. He switched off his recorder.

Lamondois reached the table and stopped.

"I have bad news for you it seems," he said slowly and evenly. "The 'charybdis' have failed." Matvei's head jerked back. "The front has been broken through north and south. The Wave is spreading and accelerating at ten metres a second. Communications with the control stations are cut. I managed to give the order to evacuate valuable instruments and records." He turned to Gorbovsky. "We're relying on you, captain. Would you tell me please what your storage capacity is?"

Gorbovsky, watching Matvei, made no reply. The director's eyes were closed. He was aimlessly smoothing the table top with his huge palms.

"Storage capacity?" repeated Gorbovsky and got up. He walked over to the control panel and bent over the microphone: "Attention, Rainbow! Navigator Falkenstein and engineer Dixon report at once to the ship."

Then he went back to Matvei and placed a hand on his shoulder.

"Not to worry, old friend. There'll be room. Give the word to evacuate the school. I'll see to the crèches."

He looked round at Lamondois. "My storage capacity isn't very large, Etienne," he said.

Etienne Lamondois' eyes were calm and dark—the eyes of a man who knew he was always right.

6

Robert saw it all happen.

He was squatting on the control tower's flat roof, carefully disconnecting the antennae. There were forty-eight of them—thin heavy spindles, mounted in a slippery parabolic frame, and every one had to be carefully unscrewed and laid away with every precaution into a special case. He was in a considerable hurry and snatched only an occasional glance over his shoulder towards the north.

Over the northern horizon towered a black wall. Along its crest, where it contacted the tropopause ran a dazzling bright edging, while higher in the empty sky pale violet lightning flickered and died. The Wave was moving inexorably but very slowly. It was hard to believe it was being held back by a thin line of clumsy machines, so tiny when seen from this height. It was oddly sultry and quiet, and the sun seemed unusually bright, as on Earth before a storm, when everything goes quiet and the sun still blazes down though half the sky is already blotted out with heavy dark-blue clouds. In this calm there was something peculiarly menacing, eerie, almost ghostly, for an advancing Wave was usually heralded by gale force winds and incessant thunder.

But now it was absolutely quiet. Robert could make out clearly the rapid voices from the square below, where they were loading into the heavy helicopter the most valuable equipment, log-books of observations, recorded data from the automatic instruments. He could hear Pagava telling someone off in his guttural tones for taking the analyzers out before necessary, while Malayev was unhurriedly discussing with Patrick the probable distribution of the charges in the energy barrier above the Wave. The whole population of Greenfield was assembled in the tower beneath Robert's feet and on the square. The rebellious biologists and two groups of tourists had been sent beyond the grain-growing areas. The biologists had been sent off in a pterocar with the lab-technicians, the latter with Pagava's orders to set up a new observation post beyond the grain belt, while a special aerobus had come from the Capital for the tourists. Both biologists and tourists had been discontented; after their departure, Greenfield contained only contented people.

Robert worked almost mechanically, and as usual when working with his hands, his mind was on other things entirely. His shoulder was hurting. Odd: he hadn't hit it on anything. His stomach was smarting—still that was only to be expected, stumbling with the ulmotron. What was that ulmotron like now? And the pterocar. And that other.... Wonder what it'll be like here in three hours time?... Pity about the flower beds. The kids worked all summer thinking up the most fantastic arrangements. I met Tanya then. "Ta-nya," he called quietly. How is she right now? He worked out the distance of the Wave front from the school. Safe, he thought, relieved. Over there I expect they don't know about the Wave, or the biologists' revolt, or my narrow escape, or Camille....

He straightened up and, wiping his brow with the heel of his palm, looked away to the south, at the endless fields of grain. He tried to picture to himself the gigantic herds of beef cattle now being driven into the heart of the continent; he thought of the labour which would be involved in re-establishing Greenfield after the Wave had spent itself, and how unpleasant it would be after two years of abundance to return to synthetic food, artificial beefsteaks, pears that tasted of tooth paste, "country soups" made of chlorella, quasibiotic mutton chops and other miracles of synthesis, rot them.... He thought of everything under the sun but he could do nothing.

There was no escaping from the surprised eyes of Pagava, Malayev's icy voice or Patrick's exaggeratedly sympathetic attitude. That was the worst thing of all—that there was simply nothing to be done. An onlooker might, to say the least, be surprised at it. Why say the least, anyway? It would look simple and that was all. A frightened observer lands all dishevelled in someone else's flyer and says his friend is dead. The friend turns out to be alive. The friend, it turns out, died afterwards, when the terrified observer made a dash for it in his flyer. But he had been crushed to death, Robert repeated to himself for the tenth time. Perhaps it was just delirium. Perhaps he had been frightened to the verge of delirium. I've never heard of that happening. Though I'd never heard of what actually happened either—if it happened. Let them think what they like, he thought, let them disbelieve him. Tanya would believe him. If only she believed him! It's all the same to them anyway, they'd forgotten about Camille at once. They'll remember him only when they see me. And they'll look at me with their theoretical eyes and they'll analyze and weigh it up. They'll construct a theory containing the fewest contradictions, and they'll never know the truth. . . . Nor will I.

He unscrewed the last antenna, laid it in the case and then put all the cases in a flat cardboard box; just then the sound of a clap came echoing down from the north, as if someone had burst a balloon in a huge empty hall. Robert turned round and saw a tall white flare burning against the slate-black background of the Wave. A "charybdis" was on fire. At once the voices below ceased while the motor of the helicopter rose to a howl and then fell to an idling note. Everybody there was no doubt straining his ears and looking towards the north. Robert had not yet grasped what had happened, when there came a shaking and rattling and the reserve "charybdis", crushing down whole palm-trees, came crawling from under the tower. It was opening its maw as it went. Out in the open it revved up till it hurt the ears, then rolled off to the north to plug the gap, wrapped in a cloud of rust and churned-up dirt.

It was nothing out of the ordinary: one of the machines hadn't managed to get rid of the excess energy into the basalt from its capacitors; Robert was just bending back to the cardboard box when something flashed bright at the foot of the black wall, a fan of multi-coloured flame burst upwards and a second pillar of white smoke climbed towards the sky, thickening and spreading as it went. Another boom came echoing back. Down below everyone was shouting together and Robert saw at once, far to the east, several more flares. The "charybdis" were bursting into flames one after another, and within a minute the eight hundred mile wall, now looking like a blackboard streaked with chalk, rocked and crawled forward, hurling black spreading blots ahead of it into the steppe. Robert swallowed with difficulty and ran down the staircase, the box under his arm.

People were pouring out into the corridors. Zina ran past him terrified, clutching some boxes and a tape to her chest. Hassan Ali-Zade and Karl Hoffmann were carrying the bulky sarcophagus containing the lab chemostaser. They headed for the door at fantastic speed. Somebody was shouting: "Come here, I can't manage it alone! Hassan...." From the entry hall came the sound of breaking glass. Motors were whining on the square outside. In the control room Pagava was jumping up and down in front of the screen, crushing maps and papers underfoot: "Why can't you hear? The 'charybdis' are on fire! On fire, I say! The Wave's here! I can't hear a thing here!... Etienne! If you've understood, nod your head!..."

Robert, wincing from the pain, hoisted the box onto his

shoulders and began the descent to the entrance hall. Behind him, someone breathing heavily was stamping down the steps. The entrance hall was scattered with wrapping paper and the wreckage of instruments. The unbreakable glass door was split down the middle. Robert squeezed out sideways and halted. He watched pterocars, loaded to the limit, lifting into the sky one after another. He saw Malayev, stony-faced and silent, cramming girl lab-assistants into the last pterocar. He watched Hassan and Karl, mouths straining open, trying to get their sarcophagus through the door of the helicopter. Somebody inside was giving them a hand and every time the sarcophagus jammed his fingers. He watched Patrick leaning against the rear light of the helicopter, calm and sleepy Patrick, his face a picture of thoughtful concentration. He turned his head and saw towering above him the coal-black wall of the Wave, blotting out the sky like a velvet curtain.

"Stop loading!" shouted Pagava in his ear. "Have you gone mad? Throw that coffin away immediately!"

The chemostaser fell back onto the concrete with a solid clang.

"Throw everything out!" yelled Pagava, running down the steps. "Everybody into the 'copter at once! Haven't you got eyes? Am I talking to the wall? Sklyarov! Patrick, you asleep?"

Robert made no move. Nor did Patrick. Meanwhile, Malayev leaned his weight against the door of the pterocar and waved his arms. The aircraft spread its wings and lurching heavily banked away behind the tower roof. Cases came flying out of the helicopter. Somebody was squealing: "I won't give it up, Shota Petrovich! I won't give them it!" "Oh, yes, you will, dear lad!" roared Pagava. "You'll give it and like it!" Malayev came running up to Pagava shouting something and pointing at the sky.

91

Robert looked up. A little observation helicopter, bristling with antennae like a hedgehog, flew over the square, his overheated engine howling like a fiend. It quickly dwindled away to the south. Pagava raised clenched fists above his head.

"Where you going?" he yelled. "Back! Back, you son of a bitch! Stop the panic! Stop him!"

All this time Robert had been standing at the top of the steps cradling the heavy cardboard box on his aching shoulder. He had the feeling he was watching a film. Now they were unloading the helicopter, that is they were throwing out everything that came to hand. The machine really was overloaded—you could tell from the sagging chassis. Round the helicopter people were crowding, at first they had been shouting, now they were quiet. Hassan was sucking his knuckles, having barked them earlier doubtless. Patrick was apparently asleep. He'd found time and what was harder, a place. Karl Hoffmann, a pedantic individual (what's called "a thoughtful and careful scientist") was catching the cases flying out of the helicopter and trying to stack them neatly—a way of keeping calm, possibly. Pagava was jumping up and down with impatience by the aircraft, glancing now at the Wave, now at the control tower. Clearly he didn't want to fly out and was regretting that he was the senior man here. Malayev was standing to one side, too, and staring fixedly at the Wave, his glance expressing cold hatred. In the shade of Patrick's old cottage my flyer is standing. I wonder who put it there and why? Nobody's paying any attention to it, it's no use to anybody either: there are ten people left at least. The helicopter's good and powerful, "griffin" type, but with a load like that it'll be able to travel at half speed. Robert laid his box down on the step.

"We won't make it," said Malayev.

His voice expressed such heart-sickness and sadness that Robert was surprised. But he knew already that they would all come through. He went up to Malayev.

"There's a reserve 'charybdis'," he said. "Will quarter of an hour do?"

Malayev looked at him uncomprehending.

"There are two reserve 'charybdis'," he said coldly and suddenly he understood.

"Right," said Robert. "Don't forget Patrick, he's on the other side of the helicopter."

Robert turned and ran. Someone shouted after him but he didn't turn round. He ran as fast as he could, leaping over discarded apparatus, over flower-beds with decorative plants, over carefully clipped bushes covered in white blossom. He was making for the western edge of the settlement. The black velvet wall hung above the houses on the right, stretching up to the zenith, while on the left blazed the blinding white sun. Robert ran past the last house and at once stumbled on the enormous rear end of a "charybdis". He glimpsed clumps of greenery caught up in the monstrous links of the caterpillar track, and bright petals torn to shreds stuck to the plates; there was a young palm-tree sticking out from between the idlers as Robert, keeping his eyes down, crawled up the narrow way into the cabin, burning his hands on the plating, grown hot in the sun. Still without raising his eyes, he wormed into the manual control cabin on his back, got into the seat and pulled the steel shade down in front of his face. Once more his hands commenced working automatically. The right hand reached out to cut in the current, the left at the same time let in the clutch and transferred control to manual, while the right was already drawing back in search of the starter button; and when everything around him began to roar, thunder and shake, his left hand pointlessly switched on the air conditioner.

Now he consciously worked the energy absorber lever, opening it to maximum, and only then let himself look forward past the shade.

Straight in front of him was the Wave. Probably no one since Liu had stood so close to the thing. It was simply black, without a break and the steppe as far as the horizon, ablaze with sunlight, was clearly outlined against it. Every blade of grass, every bush could be seen distinctly. Robert could even make out moles, little yellow pillars of frozen astonishment as they stood before their holes.

A dry whining howl started up above his head and continued to rise in volume; the absorber had begun working. The "charybdis" was rocking smoothly as it went along and the buildings of the settlement leaped in the dust of his rear mirror. There was no sign of the helicopter. Another hundred yards—no, fifty, would be enough. He sneaked a glance to his left and it seemed as if the Wave had already begun to bend back. Anyway, it was difficult to estimate what was happening. Perhaps I won't make it, he thought suddenly to himself. He couldn't take his eyes from the white columns of smoke rising beyond the horizon. The smoke was rapidly dispersing and was hard to pick out now. What was there to burn in a "charybdis"?

That's enough, he thought, braking. Otherwise I'll never get away. He took another look into the rear mirror. They're taking a long time about it, he thought. The steppe in front of the "charybdis" was slowly darkening into a huge triangle, at the apex of which stood the absorber. The moles suddenly began to jump about and one about twenty yards away fell on its back, its paws jerking convulsively.

"Get out of it, nitwits, you've still got a chance!" said Robert aloud.

94

Just then he caught sight of the second "charybdis". It stood about a quarter of a mile to the east, thirstily deploying the black throat of its absorber; before it lay an area of blackened grass, shifting in the unbearable cold.

Robert was thrilled. Great, he thought. Good man! It's not Malayev, is it? And why not? He's a man as well and all things human.... I wonder if it's Pagava himself? No, they wouldn't let him. They'd tie him up and shove him under the seat, and put their feet on him, so's he wouldn't kick. Good man! Good man! He pushed open the left-hand hatch and shouted across:

"Hey-ey! Hold on, mate! You and I'll hang on here for the rest of the year!"

He took a look at his instruments and forgot about everything else. His capacity was running out: the shining indicator under its dusty glass was hard up against the mark. He glanced swiftly into the rear mirror and felt somewhat relieved. In the white sky above the roof tops of the settlement hung a black dwindling speck. Another ten minutes, he thought. It could now be clearly seen that the Wave was bent backwards in front of the settlement and was in the process of encircling the "charybdis" from east and west.

Robert sat for a moment, gritting his teeth. All his energy was devoted to the task of driving from his mind the vision of the charred corpse in the driver's seat. If only one could switch off one's imagination.... He shook himself and took to opening all the hatches he could remember. The heavy circular one above his head. Left hatch—open wide! The right one was already opened to the limit. The door behind his back, leading to the engines ... no, better keep that one shut—the explosion would be there if anywhere, in the capacitors....

Just at that moment the other "charybdis" exploded.

Robert heard a short deafening boom, felt himself struck by a wave of hot air; he thrust his head through the hatch and saw that in his neighbour's place stood a gigantic cloud of yellow dust, covering the steppe, the sky and the Wave. In the depths of the cloud something was burning with a bright flickering flame. Something hissed through the air and bounced off the armour with a clang. Robert looked at the instruments and in one movement hurled himself out through the left-hand hatchway.

Ha fell flat on his face in the hot dry grass, picked himself up and bending double ran for the settlement. He ran like he'd never run before in his life. His "charybdis" blew up when he was already in the garden of the end house. He didn't even look round, simply hunched his shoulders, bent still lower and ran still faster. Eternal glory to you, he affirmed. Eternal glory to you!... Then he realized he'd been repeating that ever since he'd seen that terrible column of dust in place of his neighbour's "charybdis".

The square was empty, the lawns trampled, valuable, irreplaceable apparatus was lying about everywhere, cases of unique tapes, while the light wind idly ruffled the pages of unique log-books full of irreplaceable observations.

Breathing heavily, Robert cut across the square and ran up to the flyer. The engine was ticking over; in the pilot's seat, with his usual dazed look, sat Patrick.

"Well, here you are at last," said Patrick affectionately. Robert stared at him in amazement. "I'd begun to think you were staying for good. Jump in, come on, we've got to make tracks. The Wave's speed is... ."

Robert appeared beside him.

"Wait a minute," he said, out of breath. "Maybe the other one's got away as well. Who was it, Malayev? Hoffmann?"

Patrick worked the wheel clumsily, taxiing the flyer round for take-off.

"I was the other," said he shyly.

"You?"

"Me," repeated Patrick and giggled nervously. He taxied the flyer out onto the roadway and at last took it into the air. "I felt we were going to blow up so I got out and ran for it. Grand explosion, wasn't it? Rolled me as far as the houses. . . ."

The settlement slowly turned under them and slipped away. Well, Patrick, well, thought Robert astonished.

"Mine made more noise than yours when she went up," announced Patrick, "what do you think, Rob, eh?"

"Where are you heading?" asked Robert.

"Coldstream," said Patrick. "That's where the new base is going to be."

7

Robert looked over his shoulder. There was nothing now to be seen apart from the white sky and green fields. That's twice I've got away from it today, he thought, I won't make it a third time.

"What happens now?" he asked.

Patrick pursed his thick lips.

"It's going to be rough. It's got an enormous reserve of inertia by now."

"Have you tried to work it out?"

"Yes."

"Well?"

Patrick gave a heavy sigh and made no reply. Robert knitted his brows and stared straight ahead. He switched on the radio and tuned in to the school. He pressed the key several times without reply. Not to worry, he thought. Summer fête and all that. Strange, they know nothing about all this yet. Better that way, I'll be the only one to know. He put another question:

"Where are we going?"

"You've already asked once."

"Mmm ... yes, Patrick, do you need to go to this Coldstream?"

"Of course, where else is there to go?"

Robert lay back.

"Yes," he said. "A pity you stayed, really."

"What do you mean, 'pity'?"

"Can you go any faster than this?"

"I can."

"Faster still?"

Patrick was silent. The engine was gurgling, gulping in air.

"We're always in a hurry," muttered Patrick. "Always something or someone's driving us on. Faster, faster still ... can't you go a bit faster? We can, we say. Certainly!... No time to look round, no time to think. No time to go deeply into things ... why? Is it worth it? Now it's the Wave and we're in a hurry again."

"Open the throttle wider," said Robert who was thinking about something else entirely. "And hold her to the right more."

Patrick said nothing. Beneath flowed fields of ripening grain, and the occasional white buildings of the synoptic stations. They could see the cattle being driven southward straight through the wheat. The cybershepherds from this altitude looked like tiny bright stars. Their day was done.

"You've heard nothing of the 'Arrow'?" asked Robert.

"No. She's too far away to make it. Don't think about it, Rob."

"What else can I think about?" muttered Robert.

"Well, nothing. Sit yourself comfortably and have a look around. I don't know about you but I've never noticed this before. I don't think I've ever noticed the green wave the wind makes across the grain.... Wave, yes.... And you know when I first saw it? Do you really know? When I was looking through the visor on the 'charybdis'. I kept looking at that blackness and suddenly I saw the steppe and realized it was the end of everything. I was sorry for it all. And the moles were standing up and looking at the Wave and didn't understand what was going on.... You know what I discovered, Rob? Somewhere along the line we overlooked something."

Robert made no reply. A bit late to discover that, he thought. Should have done something earlier, even if it was just look out of the window.

Down below the white angles of buildings, concreted squares, and striped energy towers swam into view. It was one of the numerous energy stations in the northern belt.

"Go down," said Robert.

"Where?"

"That square over there, see it? Where the pterocars are."

Patrick glanced over the side.

"So we can land. Why?"

"Take a pterocar and leave me the flyer."

"What have you got in mind?"

"You can go on alone. I don't want to go to Coldstream. Let's get down."

Patrick obediently came in to land. He was a lousy pilot when all was said and done. Robert inspected the square.

"Excellent organization," he sneered. "Up there we're crushed to death, throw everything overboard, while here they've got three pterocars for two men."

The flyer settled clumsily between the other aircraft. Robert bit his tongue.

"Ow!" he said. "Well, come on, out you get."

Patrick quitted his seat very slowly and unwillingly.

"Rob, maybe it's none of my business, but just what are you up to?"

Robert nipped smartly into his place.

"Nothing terrible, now don't you worry. Can you manage with the pterocar?"

Patrick was standing, his hands fallen to his sides. His face was pitiful.

"Rob, be practical. There's a plasma barrier above the Wave extending for over fifty miles. You can't possibly get over that."

Robert looked at him in astonishment.

"He's dead long ago," Patrick went on. "You might have been wrong the first time but the Wave's passed over the area."

"What're you talking about?" asked Robert. "I'm not

100

aiming to get over the Wave, to Hell with it anyway. I've got something more important on hand. Good-bye. Tell Malayev I'm not coming back. Good-bye, Patrick."

"Good-bye."

"You didn't tell me whether you can cope with the pterocar or not."

"Yes, I'll manage," said Patrick sadly. "I'm used to them. Oh, Rob....."

Robert wrenched the wheel towards him and when he glanced round in five minutes the station had already vanished behind the horizon. It was two hours flying to the school. Robert checked the fuel, listened to the engine, throttled back to an economical rate of revs and cut in the automatic pilot. He tried to call up the school again. No answer. He was about to switch it off but instead let it find its own wavelength.

"...Asmodeus Barro of the ninth class found some fossils during an excursion, they resembled sea urchins. The place was quite a long way from the beach."

"...meeting at the director's. There's some odd rumours here. They say the Wave's got as far as Greenfield. Should I return to base? I don't think I've got time to do anything about the ulmotrons...."

"...couldn't put it on ourselves. We haven't got an Othello. Frankly, it seems absurd to me to put on Shakespeare. I don't think we're capable of a new interpretation, and to wait until..."

"...Vitya, are you receiving me? Fantastic news! Bullitt has decoded that gene. Get a paper and pencil. Six ... eleven ... eleven, I said...."

"Attention, Rainbow! Notice to all search parties. Begin evacuation. Special care to be taken to ensure that all aircraft of 'Medusa' class and upwards are delivered to the Capital."

"...little blue cottage right on the shore. The air's fresh

here and there's lots of wonderful sun. I never did like the Capital and I could never understand why they built it right on the equator. What? Well of course it's terribly hot. . . ."

". . .Sawyer! Sawyer! Kaneko here. Change course at once! We've already found those artists. Go south. Have a look for the third helicopter. No, it hasn't turned up yet."

"Attention, testers! At fourteen hundred today there will take place an emergency null-transportation of a man to Earth. Be at the Institute not later than thirteen hundred hours. . . ."

". . .I don't get it. I simply can't get hold of the director. All lines occupied. Do you know what's going on?"

"Adolf! Adolf! Come in, please, for Heaven's sake! Return at once, at once! There's still a chance to get aboard the spaceship!. . . (The voice began to blur, but Robert adjusted the vernier.) Terrible disaster! For some reason they're not telling anyone, but I've heard that Rainbow's doomed! Get back straight away! I want to be with you now. . . ."

Robert let fall the vernier.

". . .as usual. At Veselovsky's. No, Sinitsa's reading some new poetry. Interesting I think. I think you ought to like them. No they're not marvellous, still. . ."

". . .Why? I understand it all perfectly. Judge for yourself, 'Tariel-2' is a scout ship. Have you tried to work out how many people it can take? No, I'm staying here. Vera's decided to stay as well. It's all the same where. . ."

"Pathfinders! Pathfinders! Rendezvous—the Capital! All to the Capital! Bring your 'moles' with you, we're going to dig a shelter. We may be in time. . . ."

". . .'Tariel', you say? I know, I know, Gorbovsky. The capacity isn't much I know. Well, I suggest something of this order: Pagava from the discretes, Aristotle from the Wave-men, maybe Malayev, I'd suggest Forster from the barrier men. So he's old! He's a great man! You're only forty, my dear lad, and you've got a very poor idea of an old man's psychology. He's only got five or ten years left to live and they want to take even that away...."

"...Gabal Gabal Heard about the null-transportation? What? You're busy! What a funny man you are.... I'm off to the Institute. What d'you mean I'm mad. Yes, yes, I know all about that ... and what if it comes off just like that? Well, good-bye, look for what's left of me round Procyon."

"...The physicists have blown something up again on the North Pole. I wanted to fly up there and take a look but they've just invited us to the Capital. Oh! You as well? That's odd ... well, see you there then."

Robert turned it off. "Tariel-2" a scout ship.... He took over the controls from the automatic pilot and opened the throttle wide. Down below the grain fields came to an end and the tropical forests began. Nothing could be distinguished in the mottled yellow-green tangle, but Robert knew that under the canopy of the gigantic trees ran straight highways, now very likely bearing carloads of refugees to the west. Several freight helicopters were heading·south-west towards the horizon. Soon they were lost to view and Robert was once more alone. He grabbed his radiophone and called up Patrick. He got no reply for some time. At last Patrick's voice came through:

"Allo?"

"Patrick, it's me Sklyarov. What do we know about the Wave?"

"Nothing fresh, Rob. Pushkin shore's overrun. Aodzora's burned out. The fisheries are on fire now. Some 'charybdis' have survived and they're bringing them by tug to the Capital. Where are you now?"

"That doesn't matter. How far is it from the Wave to the school?"

"The school? Why are you worried about that? It's a long

way from there. Listen, Robert, if you're alright come to the Capital straight away. We'll all be there in half an hour." He laughed suddenly. "They tried to get Malayev aboard the spaceship. Pity you weren't here. He flattened Hassan's nose for him. And Pagava's hidden himself somewhere."

"They didn't try to get you on board?"

"Why be like that, Robert?"

"Alright, I'm sorry. So the Wave's a long way from the school?"

"Not all that far, you know. Hour, hour and a half... ."

"Thanks, Patrick, cheerio."

Robert had another try at calling up Tanya, this time by radiophone. He waited five minutes. No answer.

The school was deserted. Silence hung above the glass bedrooms, above the gardens and the many-coloured cottages. Here there was none of the panic-stricken disorder the nulls had left behind them at Greenfield. The sandy paths had been neatly swept, the desks in the garden stood as usual in even rows, the beds had been carefully made. A single doll had been abandoned in front of Tanya's cottage, and lay in the sand. Next to the doll sat a big-eyed fluffy tame kalyam. He was sniffing at her busily and glancing at Robert with good-natured curiosity.

Robert went into Tanya's room. As always it was clean and light and smelt good. An open exercise book was lying on the table and a large double towel hung on a chair. Robert put a hand on it. It was still damp. He stood by the door for a little, then absently ran his eye over the exercise book. He read his own name twice before he realized what he was doing. It was written in large block capitals.

"ROBBY! They've evacuated us in a hurry to the Capital.

Look for me there! Find me as soon as you can! They haven't told us anything yet, but it looks as if there's something awful on the way. I need you. Find me. Your T."

He tore the leaf out of the book, folded it in half and put it in his pocket. He took a last look round Tanya's room, opened the cupboard, touched her dresses, closed the door and left the cottage.

There was a good view of the sea from the cottage—it was calm like frozen green oil. Scores of paths led through the grass to the yellow beach, scattered with deck chairs and trestle beds. A number of boats were lying bottom up by the water's edge. The sun was blazing almost unbearably on the northern horizon. Robert walked quickly to his flyer. He stepped aboard, and stood still looking at the sea. Suddenly, he understood. It wasn't the sun, it was the crest of the Wave.

He sank wearily into the seat and took off. It would be the same in the south, he thought. We're hemmed in on both sides. A mouse trap. A corridor with death on both sides. He was flying again over tropical forest. Wonder how long we've got left? Two hours, three? Two places in the spaceship or ten?

The forest below petered out suddenly and Robert saw a wide clearing and a aerobus surrounded by a crowd of people. He automatically cut speed and began to lose height. The aerobus had obviously had an accident and the passengers—odd, how small they all were!—were waiting till the pilot had put the damage right. He saw the pilot, a huge black-skinned fellow with his head in the engine. Then he realized they were children and at once caught sight of Tanya. She was standing next to the pilot and taking parts as he handed them to her.

The flyer came to earth a few yards from the bus and everyone turned towards him. But Robert had eyes only for Tanya, her lovely ravaged face, her thin hands clutching the oily components to her chest, her eyes wide in astonishment.

"It's me," said Robert. "What's happened, Tanya?"

Tanya looked at him in silence. He turned to the black pilot and recognized Gaba. Gaba smiled expansively and yelled:

"Ah, Robert! Come here and give us a hand! Tanya's a marvel, but she's never had to do with an aerobus! Neither have I come to that! The engine keeps cutting out!"

The children—seven-year-old boys and girls—regarded Robert with interest. He walked up to the aerobus and looked in at the engine, lightly touching his cheek to Tanya's hair as he passed. Gaba slapped him on the back. They were old friends. They were birds of a feather—Robert and the ten bored stiff null-testers, who had been sitting for two years now with nothing to do since the failure of the experiment on Fimka, the dog.

What Robert saw in the engine made him catch his breath. Gaba had obviously never had any dealings with aerobuses. There was nothing to be done, it had run out of fuel. Gaba had taken the engine almost to pieces and all for nothing. That's what happened to the most experienced pilots sometimes: aerobuses didn't often run out of fuel. Robert stole a glance at Tanya. She was waiting with the oily bits of machinery hugged to her chest.

"Well?" asked Gaba cheerfully. "Were we right to blame this lever here, I don't know what it's called?"

"Mmm ... very possible," said Robert. He took hold of the lever and pulled at it. "Anybody knows you've come down here?"

"I told them," answered Gaba. "But they're short of vehicles there. You heard what happened to the hatcheries?"

"No, go on, what happened?" said Robert cleaning the gear lever with pointless care. He bent over so that his face couldn't be seen.

"We needed transport. Kaneko started to produce 'Medusas' but they turned automatic kitchens instead. Error in supply, eh?" Gaba roared with laughter. "How'd you like that?"

"Big laugh," said Robert through his teeth. He raised his head and looked at the sky. He saw the empty blue-white and to the north, above the distant tree-tops, the blinding bright crest of the Wave. He gently lowered the hood and muttered: "Right . . . we'll see," and walked round the bus to the side away from the rest of them. There he sank onto his haunches and pressed his forehead to the shining polished fuselage. On the other side of the bus, Gaba began to sing in a voice of gentle thunder:

> One is none, two is some,
> Three is a many, four is a penny,
> Five is a little hundred. . . .

Opening his eyes, Robert saw his dancing shadow on the grass—a shadow of lifted arms and widespread fingers. Gaba was amusing the children. Robert straightened up and climbed into the bus. A little boy was sitting in the driver's seat, hanging onto the wheel for grim death. He was doing all kinds of strange manoeuvres with it, puffing his cheeks and whistling.

"Watch it, you'll have it off," said Robert.

The boy paid no attention.

Robert had wanted to switch on the SOS beacon, but observed that it was already on. He looked at the sky again. Through the spectrolite the sky seemed a tender blue colour. It was absolutely empty. Have to make up my mind, he thought. He looked sideways at the little boy, who was imitating the roar of the wind.

"Come out here, Rob," said Gaba. He was standing by the door.

Robert climbed out.

"Close the door to."

Tanya could be heard saying something to the children on the other side of the bus, the only other sound was the lad humming and whistling in the cabin.

"When will it be here?" asked Gaba.

"Half an hour."

"What's the matter with the engine?"

"Out of fuel."

Gaba's face went grey.

"Why?" he asked pointlessly. Robert said nothing. "Has the flyer got any?"

"Wouldn't last five minutes in a tub like this."

Gaba banged his forehead with his fist and sat down on the grass.

"You're a mechanic," he said hoarsely. "Think of something."

Robert leaned against the bus.

"Remember the fairy-tale of the wolf, the goat and the cabbage? There's a dozen children here, a woman, and you and I. The woman whom I love more than anyone in the world. The woman that I'll save whatever happens. So, the flyer is a two-seater."

Gaba nodded.

"Understood. No need to say anything, of course. Let Tanya get into the flyer with as many children as she can take...."

"No," said Robert.

"Why not? They'll be in the Capital in two hours."

"No," repeated Robert. "That won't save her. The Wave'll be in the Capital in three hours. There's a spaceship waiting. Tanya's got to get away on it. Don't argue with me!" he whispered furiously. "There's only two ways. Either I fly her out or you do, but in that case you're going to swear to me by all that's holy that Tanya'll get away on that rocket! Choose."

"You're mad!" said Gaba, getting slowly up from the grass. "Remember, they're children!"

"Those that stay behind here are as well, aren't they? Who's going to pick the three to fly to the Capital and to Earth? You? Now choose."

Gaba silently opened and closed his mouth. Robert looked northwards. The Wave was now clearly visible. The shining strip was rearing ever higher dragging after it a heavy black curtain.

"Well? Do you swear?"

Gaba slowly shook his head.

"Good-bye then," said Robert.

He took a step forward, but Gaba stood in his way.

"Children," he said almost soundlessly.

Robert took him by the lapels and held his face close up against his own.

"Tanya!" he said.

For several seconds they stared into each other's eyes.

"She'll hate you for it," said Gaba quietly.

Robert set him down with a laugh.

"In three hours I'll be dead as well. It'll be all the same to me then. Good-bye, Gaba."

They parted.

"She won't go with you," said Gaba after him.

Robert made no reply. I know that, he thought. He skirted the bus and in long bounds ran toward the flyer. He saw Tanya's face turned towards him and the laughing faces of the children surrounding her. He gaily waved to them, feeling the pain in the muscles of his face as they twisted in the effort of maintaining a careless smile. He came up to the flyer, glanced inside, straightened up and shouted:

"Tanya, come and give me a hand!"

At that moment Gaba came into view on the other side of the aerobus. He was capering along on all fours.

"What are you doing idling about here?" he yelled. "Who can catch Sher-Khan, the great tiger of the jungle?"

He let out a long drawn-out roar and with a flirt of his legs in the air was away into the forest on all fours. For several seconds the children stared at him open-mouthed, then someone let out a squeal of joy, somebody else gave a war cry and the whole lot of them ran away after Gaba who was already peeping out from behind the trees.

Tanya came up to Robert, looking over her shoulder and smiling her surprise.

"Strange, isn't it?" she said. "Just as if nothing awful had happened."

Robert was still staring after Gaba. None was to be seen, but laughter, shouting, the crashing of bushes and the terrifying roar of Sher-Khan could be clearly heard.

"What a strange smile, Robert."

"Oh, he's an idiot," said Robert and at once regretted it: he should have said nothing. His voice betrayed him.

"What's happened, Rob?" asked Tanya at once.

He involuntarily looked over her head. She turned round too and pressed to him in fear.

"What's that?"

The Wave was already approaching the sun.

"We'll have to hurry," said Robert. "Nip into the cabin and lift the seat."

She leapt agilely into the cabin, then he made an immense jump after her, grabbed her right shoulder so she could not move and tore the flyer into the air.

"Robby!" whispered Tanya. "What are you doing, Robby!?"

He didn't look at her. He was busy squeezing every ounce out of the flyer. Only out of the corner of his eye could he see the green clearing below, the deserted aerobus and a little face peering out of the driver's cabin, curiously.

8

The heat was beginning to subside when the last pterocars, packed and overloaded, landed smashing their chassis on the streets adjacent to the square before the Council building. The whole population of the planet, more or less, was now gathered on this square.

From north and south grinding columns of hideous "moles" bearing the identification marks of the Pathfinders and the yellow lightning of the energy-construction corps, wound slowly into town. They came to a halt in the middle of the square and after a hasty conference, in which only two people spoke, three minutes each in low tones, it was decided to excavate a deep shelter-shaft. The "moles" began breaking through the concrete with a deafening roar, then one after another lurching foolishly from side to side they ate their way into the earth. A ring mountain of crushed earth began to rise quickly round the shaft, while the sour smell of denatured basalt hung over the square.

The deserted theatre opposite the Council building filled up with null-physicists. All day they had been on the retreat, resisting with emergency squads of "charybdis", at each observation post, each control station, saving what they could of their equipment and scientific records, risking their lives every second until direct orders came from Lamondois and the director summoning them to the Capital. They were to be recognized by their excited look which had something of guilt and challenge in it, as well as by their unnaturally lively tone of voice and their unfunny "in" jokes and their loud nervous laughter. Now, under the direction of Aristotle and Pagava they were busy selecting and photographing their most valuable material for evacuation from the planet.

A large group of mechanics and meteorologists had gone out to the limits of the town and set up production lines for small rockets. The idea was to load these rockets with the most valuable records and fire them off beyond the atmosphere as artificial satellites, so they could be picked up later and taken back to Earth. These people were joined by a number of outsiders, those who felt instinctively that they could not just sit and wait with arms folded, those who could and wanted to help and those who really believed in the necessity of saving the important documents.

Nevertheless, the square was still crowded with people as well as vehicles of every description. There were biologists and planetologists, who had lost their reason for living in the last few hours, outsiders—artists and performers—who were stunned by the unexpectedness of it all, angry and bewildered, uncertain of what to do, where to go and to whom to address their complaints. There were certain restrained and calm individuals, standing in groups between the vehicles discussing everything under the sun. And there were yet others quietly sitting in their cabins or leaning against a wall.

The planet was deserted. The entire population, every man jack had been summoned, carted and hauled out of the wildest and most distant parts of the planet to the Capital. The Capital lay on the equator and now all latitudes to north and south were empty. A few had stayed behind, saying it was all the same to them, and somewhere over the tropical forest zone an aerobus had got lost, carrying some children and their teacher—and the "griffin" sent to look for them had disappeared too.

The Council of Rainbow had been in continuous session for the past few hours under the silver spire. From time to time the voice of the director or Kaneko would call for the most unlikely people via the loudspeaker. They would run into the Council building, vanish behind the door and then race out, get into pterocars or flyers and roar out of the city. Many of those who had nothing to do followed them with envious glances. Exactly what questions were being debated by the Council remained a mystery, but the loudspeakers had already given out the main news: the threat of disaster was absolutely genuine; the Council had at its disposal a single small-capacity scout ship; the school had been evacuated and the children were now in the city park under the eyes of their teachers and doctors; the spaceliner "Arrow" was in constant touch with Rainbow and was on its way, but could not arrive in less than ten hours. Three times an hour the duty man advised the crowd of the Wave's progress. The loudspeaker growled: "Attention, Rainbow! Information bulletin. . . ." Then the square would go quiet as every one listened, straining, to the news and threw annoyed glances at the shaft, from which issued the muffled roar of the "moles". The speed of the Wave would increase—at which people would look gloomy and lower their eyes, or slow down, and then faces would light up with uncertain smiles, but the Wave never stopped, wheat fields were alight, forests flared up, deserted settlements blazed.

There wasn't much official information, mainly because there wasn't anyone to spare the time for it, and as usual in such conditions, rumours became the chief source of knowledge.

The Pathfinders and construction men burrowed ever deeper into the earth and tired, dirt-bespattered men would appear out of the shaft and shout with broad grins that in a matter of two or three hours they'd have reamed out a shelter big enough to take everybody. These men produced a kind of hope, further strengthened by persistent rumours of calculations produced by Etienne Lamondois, Pagava and somebody called Patrick. According to these calculations, when the northern and southern Waves collided at the equator, they should "interact energy-wise and deritrinitate," absorbing a considerable amount of energy. They stated that after this a four-foot layer of snow should fall on Rainbow.

There was talk that a half hour before, in the Discrete Space Institute whose white, windowless walls were in full view of the square, they had succeeded in sending a man to the solar system by null-transport, and they'd even given out the name of the pilot, the first null-pilot ever, at this moment it was said, safely on Pluto.

People talked of signals received from behind the southern Wave. They were heavily distorted but were nevertheless deciphered and it turned out, that a number of people who had volunteered to stay behind on one of the energy stations in the track of the Wave, had survived and felt no ill effects, which was taken to be proof that the P-Wave as distinct from earlier types of Wave, did not constitute a real hazard to life. Even the names of the survivors were mentioned and there were people to be found who had known them personally. To back this up the story went round of a man who had seen with his own eyes the celebrated Camille hurtling through the Wave in a blazing pterocar, shouting something and waving his arms as he swept past like a great comet.

One rumour which achieved wide currency came from one old spaceman, now working down the shaft, who was reported to have said something to this effect: "I've known the captain of the 'Arrow' for donkeys' years. If he says he won't be here sooner than ten hours, that means he'll be here in three hours at the latest. Don't pay any attention to the Council. They're a bunch of amateurs in there—they've got no idea of what a modern spaceship can do in expert hands."

The world had suddenly lost its simplicity and clarity. It had got difficult to sort out truth from lies. Your trusted

114

childhood friend could cheerfully deceive you, in the hope of calming you and cheering you up, and you'd find him twenty minutes later in misery over some rubbishy rumour that the Wave, though not dangerous to life did have ineradicable effects on a man's mind, reducing it to caveman level.

The people on the square saw a tall, well-built woman, her face tear-stained, go into the Council building, leading a five-year-old youngster in red shorts by the hand. Many of them recognized her as the wife of the director, Zhenya Vyazanitsyna. She came out quickly in the company of Kaneko, who held her elbow politely but firmly. She was no longer crying but her face had an expression of such fierce determination that people made way for her in alarm. The lad calmly chewed on a biscuit.

Those who had something to occupy themselves with were a good deal better off. With this in mind, a considerable group of writers and artists, after arguing till they were hoarse, came to a firm decision and moved off to the outskirts of the town to help the rocket men. They could hardly hope to be of serious use but they were confident they would be given something to do. Some went down the shaft, where horizontal work was already in progress. A number of experienced pterocar pilots took off for north and south to give a hand to the Council's observers who had for several hours now been playing hide and seek with death.

The ones who stayed behind saw a charred flyer, covered in dirt and dents, come down in front of the Council building. Two figures crawled out, tottered for a moment on shaky legs and headed for the door, holding one another up. Their faces were yellow and swollen and it was with difficulty that the onlookers made out the features of the young physicist Karl Hoffmann and the null-experimenter, Timothy Sawyer, the celebrated banjo player. Sawyer just shook his head and mumbled, Hoffmann, clearing his throat several times, recounted indistinctly that they had just been trying to fly over the Wave and had approached to within twelve miles of it when Tim's eyes went queer and they had been forced to turn back. The idea had been put forward in the Council, evidently, for an attempt to be made to transfer the population over the Wave. Sawyer and Hoffmann had been scouts. At that point someone said that two Pathfinders were trying to burrow under the Wave in the sea, using an experimental bathyscaphe. They hadn't returned yet and nothing had been heard from them.

About two hundred people were now left on the square by now—less than half of the adult population of Rainbow. They tried to keep together in groups, and talked slowly among themselves, not taking their eyes off the Council windows. It had grown quiet on the square: the "moles" had gone deep and their roar was barely heard. The conversations were not cheerful.

"My holiday's spoilt again. This time for quite a while, it seems."

"Shelters, dug-outs, underground ... the black wall has come again and people are going underground."

"Pity I don't feel in the least like painting. Look how beautiful the Council building is. Such depth of colour. I'd love to get it all down on canvas and get across the feeling of strain and expectation, but I can't. I feel sick."

"It's funny, all the same. We didn't elect a secret Council, after all. High priests! Shut themselves up in the chamber there and decide the fate of the planet. I'm not all that worried what they're discussing in there, but it's not right. . . ."

"I don't like the look of Ananyev at all. Fancy he's been sitting there on his own for two hours now, not talking to anyone, just sharpening his knife. I'm going over to talk to him. You coming?"

116

"Aodzora's gone up in flames ... my Aodzora. I built it. Now I'll have to build it over again...and they'll burn it again."

"I'm sorry for them. Here we are together and honestly I'm not frightened a bit! But Matvei Sergeyevich can't be with his wife even in the last hours. All this is stupid. Why?"

"I sit here and natter because this is what I reckon: the only hope is the spaceship. All the rest is tripe, amateur theatricals."

"Why did I come here? Why didn't I stay on Earth? Rainbow, how you've let us down!"

The loudspeaker again:

"Attention, Rainbow! Council speaking! All personnel to a full meeting of the population! The meeting will take place on the main square in twenty minutes. I repeat..."

As he was pushing through the crowd towards the Council building Gorbovsky became aware that he was a highly popular man. People gave way before him, he was pointed out by eyes and even fingers, people greeted him and asked: "How are things going, Leonid Andreyevich?"—behind his back they pronounced his name in an undertone, the names of the stars and planets he had had anything to do with, and the names of the ships he had commanded. Gorbovsky hadn't been used to such popularity for a long time; he bowed in all directions, saluted, smiling and answering: "Yes, everything's okay"—and thought: Now let somebody tell me the mass of people aren't interested in space travel. At the same time he was almost physically conscious of the terrific nervous tension present on the square. It was something like the last minutes before a very difficult and important examination. The strain communicated itself to him. Smiling and joking, he tried to estimate the mood and collective will of this crowd and guessed what

117

they would say when he announced his decision. I believe in you, he thought persistently. I believe in you whatever happens. I believe in you, frightened, cautious, disappointed fanatics. People.

By the door, a stranger in a miner's outfit overtook him.

"Leonid Andreyevich," he said smiling anxiously. "A moment, please, really just one moment."

"By all means," said Gorbovsky.

The man rummaged in his pockets hastily.

"When you get to Earth," he went on, "do me a favour, please.... Where the devil it got to? I don't think it'll be too much trouble for you. Ah, here it is...." He took out an envelope folded in two. "The address is in block letters ... say you'll send it."

Gorbovsky gave a nod.

"I could send it even if the address were in handwriting," he said gently, taking the envelope.

"My handwriting's lousy. I can't read it myself and I've just written this in a hurry..." he stopped and thrust out his hand. "Good trip! Thanks in advance."

"How's your shaft getting on?"

"Fine. Don't you worry about us."

Gorbovsky went on into the Council building and as he went up the stairway he thought over the first sentence of his speech to the assembly. He couldn't seem to get it right.

He was just coming up to the first floor when he saw that the members of the Council were coming down. Lamondois was first, stepping lightly and trailing his fingers along the banister; he was completely calm and even looked a bit absent-minded. On seeing Gorbovsky, he smiled a strange, wild smile and lowered his eyes at once. Gorbovsky stood to one side. Behind Lamondois came the director, fiercely purple. "You ready?" he growled and passed on without waiting for an answer. Then followed the rest of the Council with whom Gorbovsky was not acquainted. They were loudly engrossed in an animated discussion on the construction of an entrance to the underground shelter, the loudness and liveliness reeked of falsity and it was very clear their minds were on something else. Last of all, and some way behind came Stanislav Pishta, the same broad, bushy-haired, deeply tanned Pishta as twenty-five years before, when he commanded the "Sunflower" and with Gorbovsky conquered the Blind Spot.

"Boo!" said Gorbovsky.

"Oh!" said Stanislav Pishta.

"What are you doing here?"

"Quarrelling with the physicists."

"Good lad," said Gorbovsky. "I'm going to as well. But before that tell me who looks after the children's colony?"

"I do," answered Pishta.

Gorbovsky looked at him mistrustfully.

"I do! I do," Pishta grinned. "Don't you believe me? You will in a minute. On the square. When the argument starts. I can tell you, it'll be a decidedly uneducational sight."

They were slowly going down to the exit.

"Let them argue. That's nothing to do with you. Where are the kids?"

"In the park."

"Excellent. Get over there and start loading the children on board the 'Tariel', got it? At once, mind, straight away. Mark and Percy will be there. We've already got the crèches aboard. Get cracking."

"Good man," said Pishta.

"And now," said Gorbovsky. "Run."

Pishta slapped him on the back and took the stairs three at a time. Gorbovsky followed. He saw hundreds of faces turned towards him and heard the booming voice of Matvei speaking into the megaphone:

"...so in fact we're deciding the question now what is

most important for humanity and for us as part of humanity. The first to speak will be the director of the childrens' colony, Stanislav Pishta."

"He's gone," said Gorbovsky.

The director looked round.

"What d'you mean?" he whispered. "Where?"

It was very quiet on the square.

"Well, let me then," said Lamondois. He grabbed the megaphone.

Gorbovsky saw his thin white fingers gripping the director's thick fingers tensely clenched. The director unwillingly gave up the megaphone.

"We all know what Rainbow is," began Lamondois. "Rainbow is a planet colonized by science and designed for physical experiments. All mankind is waiting for the results of these experiments. Each person who comes to Rainbow, and lives here, knows where he has come and where he lives." Lamondois spoke sharply and confidently, he was very fine now, pale, erect, tense as a string. "We are all soldiers of science. We have given up our lives to science. We have given her all our love and the best that is in us. What we have created belongs really not to us. It belongs to science and to all the twenty thousand million Earthmen scattered about the universe. To talk on moral themes is always hard, and unpleasant. Too often our reason and logic is hindered by our purely emotional 'I want' or 'I don't want' or 'I like it' or 'I don't like it'. But an objective law exists which is the motive force of human society. It doesn't depend on our emotions. It states: mankind must find out. That is the main thing for us—the struggle of knowledge against ignorance. And if we don't want our actions to seem ridiculous in the light of that law, then we must follow it, even if this means jettisoning certain ideas we have been born with or have been brought up to believe in." Here he stopped and unbuttoned his shirt. "The most valuable thing on Rainbow is our work. We have been studying discrete space for thirty years. We have collected here the finest null-physicists in the world. The ideas thrown up by our work are still in the process of being studied, so profound are they, so full of potential, overall so paradoxical. I am not exaggerating when I say that only here on Rainbow are there people in existence who have a new conception of space, and only here exists the experimental data essential to the working out of this conception. But even we, the specialists, can't forecast the enormous, gigantic power our new theory will bring to man over his world. In any case science will be thrown back not thirty years—a hundred, two, three hundred years. . . ."

Lamondois stopped, his face red and blotchy, his shoulders sagged. A dead silence hung over the town.

"I very much want to live," said Lamondois suddenly. "And the children . . . I've two of my own, a boy and a girl; they're there in the park. . . . I don't know. You decide."

He let fall the megaphone and remained standing in front of the crowd, limp, old and pitiful.

The crowd was silent. The null-physicists standing in the front rows, unhappy bearers of the new conception of space, said nothing. The artists and performers, who well knew what thirty years of work meant and too well knew that no masterpiece was repeatable, said nothing. The construction engineers who had worked thirty years side by side with the nulls said nothing as they sat on piles of excavated earth. The Council members, those reckoned to be the cleverest, the wisest and the kindest of men and on whom the final decision here depended, said nothing.

Gorbovsky saw hundreds of faces, young and old, of men and women, and they all looked the same to him,

121

they all had an extraordinary resemblance to that of Lamondois. He could imagine their thoughts with the utmost clarity. The young wanted to live because they had lived for only a short while. The old wanted to live because only a short time remained to them. They all wanted to live. A man could cope with this: an effort of will and it could be driven down into the depths of the mind, swept aside. Those who couldn't manage that, put all their energy and thought into not betraying their deathly terror. The rest ... a pity about the work. A terrible pity about the children, unbearable—there were plenty of people present who cared nothing for children but thought it swinish to think about anything else. And the decision must be made. God, what a decision! You had to choose and say aloud what you had chosen. And at the same time take upon yourself a huge responsibility, a quite unaccustomed responsibility before yourself, so that the last three hours of your life you could feel yourself to be a man, and not be bent under a weight of unbearable shame and not waste your last breath shouting "fool! swine!" at yourself. Mercy, decided Gorbovsky.

He went up to Lamondois and took the megaphone from him. Lamondois didn't seem to notice.

"You see," Gorbovsky's piercing voice came through the megaphone, "I'm afraid there's been some misunderstanding here. Lamondois is asking you to decide. But, you see, there's really nothing to decide. Everything's been decided. The crèches and the new-born babies and their mothers are already aboard the ship. (The crowd sighed noisily.) The rest of the children are embarking now. I think there's room for them all. In fact, I know there is. I hope you'll forgive me for deciding the matter independently. I have the right to do that. I even have the right to prevent all attempts to stop me carrying out this decision. But that's by the way. In general Lamondois mentioned some interesting ideas. I'd like to argue with him but I've got to go. Entry to the spaceport is open to all parents. I'd rather you didn't go on board, I'm sorry."

"That's it then," said somebody loudly in the crowd. "And so it should be. Miners, follow me!"

The crowd started to break up noisily. Some pterocars took off.

"Basically speaking," said Gorbovsky, "the most valuable thing we have is our future... ."

"We haven't got one," said a harsh voice in the crowd.

"Oh yes, you have! Our future is the children. That's a really new thought, isn't it? Anyway we've got to be fair. Life is wonderful, and we all know that. The children don't know that yet. How much they've yet got to come if we think just about love! Not to mention null-problems!" (Some applause from the crowd here.) "Now I must go."

Gorbovsky thrust the megaphone onto one of the Council members and made his way over to Matvei. Matvei slapped him hard on the back several times. They looked at the melting crowd and at the enlivened faces which had suddenly become different from one another. Gorbovsky murmured with a sigh:

"It's funny really. Here we are perfecting ourselves all the time, getting better and better, wiser and kinder, and yet how very pleasant it is, after all, when somebody takes a decision for us."

9

"Tariel 2" was a Sigma-D class spaceship designed to carry small groups of researchers with a minimum of laboratory equipment over great distances. She was excellent for landing on planets with turbulent atmospheres and possessed tremendous acceleration; she was tough and reliable and ninety-five per cent of her was made up of energy capacitors. Consequently, the living quarters of the ship consisted of five tiny cabins, a tiny ward-room, a miniature galley, together with a control room stuffed with control panels and steering equipment. The vessel also contained a freight compartment—quite a spacious area this, with bare walls and a low ceiling; it lacked air conditioning but it could, in a real emergency, serve as a makeshift laboratory. Under normal conditions "Tariel 2" could take up to ten men, including the crew.

The children were embarked through both hatches: the younger ones went through the passenger hatch and the older ones via the freight opening. People crowded round both entrances and there were a lot more than Gorbovsky expected. It was obvious from the first that there weren't just parents and teachers present. Some distance away were piled-up cases of undistributed ulmotrons and equipment for the Pathfinders of Lalanda. The adults were quiet but there was a considerable noise round the ship: squeals, laughter, some thin voices raised in faltering song—the hubbub typical of all the kindergartens and infant schools that ever were. Gorbovsky couldn't see anybody he knew except for Alya Postysheva standing a bit to one side. And even she was quite different—slumped and sad, dressed neatly and with taste. She was sitting on an empty case with her hands on her knees, looking at the ship. She was waiting.

Gorbovsky climbed out of the pterocar and headed for the ship. As he was passing Alya she smiled pitifully at him and said: "I'm waiting for Mark." "Yes indeed, he'll be out in a minute," said Gorbovsky gently and pressed on. He soon realized that getting to the hatch wasn't going to be all that easy.

A large bearded man in a panama barred his path.

"Gorbovsky, take this, I beg you."

He handed over a long heavy parcel.

"What is it?" asked Gorbovsky.

"It's my last painting. I am Jogan Surd."

"Jogan Surd," repeated Gorbovsky. "I didn't know you were here."

"Take it, it doesn't weigh much. It's the best thing I've ever done. I brought it here for the exhibition. It's called **The Wind... .**"

Gorbovsky felt all screwed up inside.

"Alright, then," and took the parcel carefully.

Surd bowed.

"Thank you, Gorbovsky," he said and vanished in the crowd.

Someone seized painful hold on Gorbovsky's arm. He turned and saw a young woman. Her lips were trembling and her face was wet with tears.

"Are you the captain?" she asked in a broken voice.

"Yes, yes, I'm the captain."

She gripped his arm even more painfully.

"My boy's there. On the ship..." her lips started to curve downward. "I'm afraid... ."

Gorbovsky made an astonished face.

"What on earth for? He's absolutely safe in there."

"You're sure, you promise?"

"He's absolutely safe there," repeated Gorbovsky decisively, "it's a grand ship!"

"So many children," she said, sobbing. "So many children..."

She let fall her arm and turned away. Gorbovsky tapping his foot in hesitation, set off again, protecting Surd's masterpiece with his hands and chest, but was grabbed by the elbow from both sides at once.

"It only weighs six pounds," said a pale angular individual. "I have never asked anyone for anything in my life...."

"I can see that," agreed Gorbovsky. And he spoke no more than the truth.

"It's the record of Wave observations over ten years. Six million photographs."

"It's extremely important!" confirmed the second man, holding Gorbovsky by the left elbow. He had thick kindly lips, his cheeks were unshaven and his little eyes were imploring. "You realize this is Malayev...." He pointed at the first man. "You must take it at once...."

"Shut up a minute, Patrick," said Malayev. "Leonid Andreyevich, please understand ... it's so that never again," he caught his breath, "so that nobody will ever need to present such a disgraceful choice to us again...."

"Carry it for me. I've got my hands full."

They let go of him and he took a step forward and straight away banged his knee on something big wrapped in tarpaulin; two boys in identical blue berets were holding it with obvious difficulty.

"Can you take it?" panted one.

"If you can," said the other.

"We've been building it two years...."

"Please."

Gorbovsky shook his head and began to pick his way round them carefully.

"Leonid Andreyevich," said the first plaintively. "We beg you."

Gorbovsky shook his head again.

"Don't grovel," said the second angrily. He suddenly let go his corner and the swathed object fell to the ground with a crash. "What're you holding it for?"

With unexpected fury he kicked his machine and went off limping heavily.

"Volodya!" shouted the first after him, in some alarm. "Don't go mad!"

Gorbovsky turned away.

"Sculptors have no hope at all, of course, have they?" said a conspiratorial voice above his ear.

Gorbovsky only shook his head: he was unable to speak. Behind his back, treading on his heels came Malayev, breathing hoarsely.

Yet another group of people with spools, parcels and packets moved at once from their places and paced alongside him.

"Maybe we should do it this way," began one of them, nervous and hesitant. "Pile everything up by the freight hatch. We realize there's not a lot of chance ... but perhaps there'll be a little room, who knows ... it's things, after all, not people ... stick them anywhere ... somehow...."

"Yes ... yes," said Gorbovsky. "Do that." He slowed down and shifted Surd's masterpiece to the other shoulder. "Tell everyone to do that. Put all the stuff by the freight hatch. To the side and ten paces off, okay?"

The crowd began to thin out, as people dispersed in the direction indicated by Gorbovsky, and he soon emerged in an open space in front of the passenger hatch, where little boys and girls, standing in twos, were waiting their turn to fall into the hands of Percy Dixon.

The toddlers in their vari-coloured jackets, pants and caps were in a state of joyous excitement, brought about by the prospect of a real flight in a spaceship. They were much preoccupied with each other and the huge light-blue ship, and could spare only the most fleeting glances for the crowd of parents milling below. They had no time for parents. In the round hatch stood Percy Dixon, arrayed in an ancient long-forgotten spaceman's parade uniform, heavy and stifling, with silvered buttons, badges and blinding braid all over the place. Sweat poured down his hairy face and from time to time he would roar out in a nautical voice: "Man the t'gallants! Stand by to weigh anchor!" It was very gay and the adoring boys couldn't take their eyes off him. There were two staff there as well: the man was holding some lists in his hand while the woman was singing a cheerful song with the children about a brave rhinoceros. The little lads, their eyes fixed on Dixon, sang the refrains with great abandon, each sticking to his own melody.

Gorbovsky was thinking that if you stood like this with your back to the crowd, you could easily think that good old Uncle Percy was organizing a jolly trip round Rainbow for the kiddies in a real spaceship. Just then, however, Dixon lifted the next child up in his arms and turned to hand him to someone in the hatch and a woman's voice behind Gorbovsky's back cried out hysterically: "Tolik! My Tolik...." Gorbovsky looked round and saw Malayev's pale face and the strained faces of the fathers and mothers, smiling their pitiful crooked smiles, tears standing in their eyes, the bitten lips, the despair, and the hysterical woman who was being hurriedly led away by a man in an earth-stained boiler suit. His arm was about her shoulders. One person turned away, another quickly made off blundering into the bystanders, another just lay down on the concrete and buried his head in his hands.

Gorbovsky caught sight of Zhenya Vyazanitsyna, plumper and prettier than when he had last seen her, with huge dry eyes and mouth clamped tight. She held the hand of a fat unexcited little boy in red shorts. The lad was munching an apple and his eyes were fixed on the resplendent Percy Dixon.

"Hello, Leonid," said she.

"Hello, Zhenya, my dear," said Gorbovsky.

Malayev and Patrick went off to one side.

"My, how thin you are," she said. "Still as thin as ever. And even more dried up."

"You've got prettier."

"I'm not stopping you working?"

"No, of course not. Everything's going like clockwork. I've only got to look the ship over. I'm still very much afraid we're not going to have enough room."

"It's so hard to cope on my own. Matvei's busy all the time. I sometimes think he doesn't give a hang."

"That's just not true," said Gorbovsky. "I've spoken to him. I know: it's just the opposite with him.... But there's nothing he can do. All the children on Rainbow are his children. He can't do otherwise."

She gestured with her free hand.

"I don't know what to do with Alyosha," said she. "He's used to living at home. He's never even been to the kindergarten."

"He'll get used to it. Children get used to things very fast, Zhenya. And don't you worry, he'll be alright."

"I don't even know who to talk to about him."

"All the staff are good. You know yourself they're all the same. Alyosha'll get along okay."

"I don't mean that. He's not on any of the lists, you know."

"What's so terrible about that? List or not, no child is staying on Rainbow. The lists are just so that we don't lose track of the kids. I'll tell them to put his name down if you like."

"Yes, alright ... no, wait a minute. Perhaps I could take him up into the ship myself?"

Gorbovsky shook his head sadly.

"Zhenya, I wouldn't. It'll only disturb the children."

"I shan't disturb anyone. I only want to see what it'll be like for him there, who'll be sitting next to him...."

"Kids like him. Happy and good-natured."

"Can I go up with him?"

"Don't, Zhenya."

"I have to, I really have to. He won't be able to get on by himself. How can he live without me? You just don't understand. None of you understand me. I shall do what has to be done. Any sort of work. I can do anything, you know. Don't be so heartless."

"Zhenya, take a look around you. They're all mothers."

"He's not the same as the rest. He's weak and has tantrums. He's used to constant attention. He can't get on without me, he can't! I ought to know that better than anybody, surely! You're not going to take advantage of the fact that I can't complain to anyone about you?"

"Surely you wouldn't take the place of a child who would have to stay on Rainbow?"

"Nobody's going to stay behind," she said passionately. "I'm sure of it! They'll all find a place! I don't need a place! Some corner of the engine room, a cubby hole.... I've got to be with him!"

"I can't do anything for you, I'm sorry."

"You can! You're the captain, you can do anything. You were always a kind man, Lenya!"

"I'm being kind now. You've no idea just how kind I'm being."

"I'm not going to leave you," she said and said no more.

"Alright, let's do it like this. I'll take Alyosha on board and come back to you. Okay?"

She looked him straight in the eyes.

"You're not telling me lies. I can tell. I believe you. You've never deceived anyone."

"I won't let you down. When the ship blasts off you'll be next to me. Give me the boy."

Not taking her eyes off his face, as if in a dream she pushed Alyosha towards him.

"Go on, Alik," she said. "Go with Uncle Lenya."

"Where?" asked the boy.

"Into the ship," said Gorbovsky, taking his hand. "Where else did you think? Into this ship, to this nice man here. Want to?"

"I want to, to that man," announced the boy. He didn't look at his mother any more.

They went up to the gangway, up which the last of the children were making their way. Gorbovsky addressed the member of staff:

"Put him on the list. Alexei Matveyevich Vyazanitsyn."

The man looked at the boy and then at Gorbovsky and nodded, writing. Gorbovsky slowly mounted the gangplank, handing Alexei Matveyevich over the high coaming.

"This is called the lock," said he.

The boy pulled himself free and went right up to Percy Dixon and began to inspect him. Gorbovsky put Surd's picture in a corner. What else? he thought, oh yes! He went back to the hatch, poked his head out and took Malayev's briefcase.

"Thank you," said Malayev, smiling. "You didn't forget. . . ."

Patrick was smiling as well. Nodding, they stumbled back into the crowd. Zhenya was standing right under the hatch and Gorbovsky waved to her. He turned to Dixon.

"Hot?"

"Hellish. Oh for a shower right now. But there's children in there."

"Well, clear the shower cubicles."

"Easier said than done," Dixon sighed heavily and bent over to loosen the neck of his thick tunic.

"My beard keeps getting under the collar," he mumbled. "Prickles like anything."

"Mister," said Alyosha. "Is your beard real?"

"Pull it if you like," said Percy with a sigh and bent down.

The boy pulled on it.

"It's still not real," he announced.

Gorbovsky took him by the shoulder but the lad squirmed free.

"I don't want to go with you," said he. "I want to go with the captain."

"Fair enough," said Gorbovsky. "Percy, take him to the teacher."

He strode over to the door leading in to the corridor.

"Don't throw a fit," said Percy to his back.

Gorbovsky rolled the door aside. Indeed the ship had never seen the like. There was squealing and laughing, whistling and twittering, cooing and war-cries, knocking, ringing, stamping, the scrape of metal on metal, the mewling of tiny babies... the unique blend of smells—milk, honey, medicines, overheated childrens' bodies, soap, all this despite the air-conditioning and the emergency ventilators which were working at full blast.... Gorbovsky picked his way along the corridor, fearfully peeping into open doors where forty or more boys and girls between two and six were jumping and dancing, nursing dolls, aiming rifles, throwing lassos. Crowded together indescribably tightly, they sat and crawled on the open bunks, on the tables, under the tables and under the bunks. The harassed teachers ran from cabin to cabin; in the ward-room, now stripped of its furniture, young mothers fed and dressed their babies alongside the crèche—five crawlers chattering to one another in bird language and wandering about on all fours in a fenced-off corner. Gorbovsky thought what it would all be like in free fall, frowned and walked through into the control room.

He couldn't recognize it. It was bare. The huge control panel which had occupied a third of the space had gone. The pilot's controls had disappeared along with the second pilot's chair. The view-screen desk had disappeared. The chair in front of the computer had gone and the computer itself, half dismantled, displayed its shining innards. The ship was no longer a spaceship. It had turned into an interplanetary barge, with plenty of speed but good only for flights on inertia trajectories.

Gorbovsky thrust his hands into his pockets. Dixon was breathing in his ear.

"Well, well," said Gorbovsky. "Where's Falkenstein?"

"Here." Falkenstein poked his head out from the depths of the computer. He was grim and determined.

"Good lad, Mark," said Gorbovsky. "And you as well, Percy, thank you."

"Pishta's been asking for you three times already," said Mark and returned to the computer. "He's by the freight hatch."

Gorbovsky crossed the control room and came out into the transport section. He went hot and cold. Here in the long and narrow hold, feebly lit by two gas lamps, stood the school boys and girls of all ages, pressed tightly against one another. They stood quiet, barely moving, just shifting from one foot to the other, looking out of the open hatch where the blue sky could be glimpsed along with the flat roof of the distant warehouse. Biting his lip, Gorbovsky looked at the children for several seconds.

"Take the first years into the corridor," he said. "Second and third into the control room. Now."

"That's not all," said Dixon quietly. "There's ten stuck somewhere on the way from the school.... Well, I expect they've had it by now. One bunch of seniors are refusing to embark. There's another group of outsider children who've just arrived. Anyway, you'll see for yourself."

"All the same, you do what I said," suggested Gorbovsky. "First three forms into the corridor and control room. Here light, a screen, show some films. Historical films. Let them see what it was like before. Get moving, Percy. And another thing, get the lads to make a chain to Falkenstein so they can get the valves and things out—it'll keep them occupied a bit."

He made his way to the hatch with difficulty and ran down.

At the foot of the gangway surrounded by teachers, stood a large group of children of various ages. On the left were strewn in an untidy heap the most valuable items of the material culture of Rainbow; bundles of documents, briefcases, machines and models of machines, sculptures wrapped up in cloth. To the right and about twenty paces off stood some gloomy boys and girls aged about fifteen or sixteen; Stanislav Pishta was pacing up and down in front of them, very serious, his hands behind his back, eyes fixed on the ground. He was speaking quietly:

"Think of it as an exam. Think less of yourselves and a bit more about others. And what's there to be ashamed about? Take a hold on yourselves and you'll stop feeling that way!"

The seniors kept a stubborn silence. The adults crowded round the hatch were crushed into silence too. Some of the boys stole glances around them and it was obvious that they were contemplating flight. This however was out of the question, their parents were standing all round them. Gorbovsky looked at the hatch. Even from here it was clear that the ship was bursting at the seams. Children were standing in tight ranks in the wide entrance. Their faces were not those of children, they were too serious and too sad.

134

A huge and handsome young man somehow came up to Gorbovsky sideways. His sad eyes looked a request, grotesquely inappropriate in that face.

"One word, captain," he brought out in a quavering voice. "Just one word."

"Just a moment," said Gorbovsky.

He went over and put his arms round Pishta's shoulders.

"There are places for everyone," Pishta was saying. "Don't worry about that."

"Stanislav," said Gorbovsky, "get the rest on board."

"There's no room there," objected Pishta with supreme inconsistency. "We were waiting for you. It would be a good idea to clear out the reserve D-chamber."

"There aren't any reserve D-chambers on the 'Tariel'. There'll be room though. Go and see."

Gorbovsky stayed face to face with the senior pupils.

"We don't want to go," offered one of them, a mature tow-haired lad with bright green eyes. "The teachers ought to go."

"That's right!" said a little girl in a track suit.

Behind them Percy's voice could be heard shouting:

"Throw it out, straight onto the ground!"

The circuit plates rang as they sprayed out of the hatch. The conveyer had started to work.

"Look here, boys and girls," said Gorbovsky. "First of all, you haven't got the right to vote because you haven't left school yet. And secondly you ought to listen to your conscience. You're still young, of course, and you long to do great deeds, but the plain fact is here you're not wanted—you're wanted aboard ship. I shudder to think what it'll be like in there during free fall. Two senior pupils are needed in each cabin to look after the infants and at least three sharp girls for the crèche and to help the mothers with the little babies. In short, that's where you're asked to be heroes."

135

"Excuse me, captain," said green-eyes witheringly, "but all these duties could be carried out by the teachers quite well."

"Excuse me, young man," said Gorbovsky, "I suppose you are familiar with the rights of the captain. As captain I assure you that out of the teachers only two are going. And this is the main thing, just think how your teachers would live in the future with the knowledge that they've taken your places. The games are over, boys and girls, you've got a life in front of you, a kind of life that happens, fortunately, rarely. And now you must excuse me, I'm busy. As consolation I can only say one thing: you'll be the last to go on board. That's all!"

He turned his back on them and walked into the young man with the pleading eyes.

"Oh, I'm sorry, I completely forgot about you."

"You said that two teachers were going," he said hoarsely. "Who?"

"Who are you?" asked Gorbovsky.

"I'm Robert Sklyarov. I'm a null-physicist. But it's not about me. I'll tell you all about it in a minute, but first of all tell me who of the teachers is going?"

"Sklyarov... Sklyarov... strangely familiar. Where've I heard it?"

"Camille," said Sklyarov, forcing a smile.

"Ah," said Gorbovsky. "So you're interested in who's going?" He looked hard at Sklyarov. "Alright, I'll tell you. Only you though. The man in charge of the children and the chief doctor. They don't know that yet."

"No," said Sklyarov, grabbing hold of Gorbovsky's hands. "One more, just one more. Tatyana Turchina. She's a teacher there. They all like her. She's terribly experienced."

Gorbovsky freed his hands.

"No," said he. "Can't be done, my dear Robert! Only

children and mothers with new-born babies are going, you see? Only children and mothers with breast babies."

"Her as well!" said Sklyarov at once. "She's a mother too! She's going to have a baby...my baby...she's a mother as well!"

Gorbovsky felt something hit his shoulder forcibly. He staggered and saw Sklyarov falling back in alarm, giving way as a small thin woman, astonishingly elegant and slim, her golden hair heavily streaked with grey, came towards him, her lovely face a mask of stone. Gorbovsky rubbed his hand across his brow and went back to the gangway.

Only the seniors and the teachers were still left here. The rest of the adults, that is the fathers and mothers and those who had brought their works of art, and those who had trailed along to the ship with vague unconscious hopes, fell back slowly, splitting into groups. Stanislav Pishta stood in the hatchway, his legs apart:

"Squeeze up a bit more, lads! Michael, shout to them in the control room to squeeze up! Bit more!"

Serious youthful voices came back:

"We can't! There's no more room. Everybody's standing close together!"

Then Percy's thick voice rumbled:

"What d'you mean, no room? What about here behind the panel? Don't be frightened, you won't get a shock, pass along, pass along...you as well, and you pugnose...that's the way...."

And the cold, ringing voice of Falkenstein, like iron, could be heard:

"Squeeze up, lads...let's past ... move over, lass... gangway, lad...."

Pishta moved to one side and Falkenstein appeared next to him with his jacket over his shoulder.

"I'm staying on Rainbow," he said. "You'll get by without

me, Leonid Andreyevich." His eyes roamed the crowd, searching for someone.

Gorbovsky nodded.

"Is the doctor on board?" he asked.

"Yes," answered Mark. "Only adults there are the doctor and Dixon."

A burst of laughter came from the hatch.

"That's the way to do it ... one-two, one-two."

Dixon appeared in the hatchway above Pishta's head, his upside-down face sweaty and bright-red.

"Catch me, Leonid," he hissed. "I'll fall in a minute."

The children laughed out loud. It was really a funny sight: the fat flight mechanic was hanging on the ceiling like a fly, his fingers and feet crooked round the brackets used for securing the cargo. He was hot and heavy; when Pishta and Gorbovsky pulled him out and set him on his feet, he said, breathing heavily:

"Old. I'm old...."

Blinking guiltily, he glanced at Gorbovsky.

"I can't go in there, Leonid. It's hot, stifling, packed-out ... this cursed uniform.... I'm staying here, you go with Mark. I'm sick of you both anyway."

"Good-bye, Percy," said Gorbovsky.

"'Good-bye, old friend," said Dixon, touched.

Gorbovsky burst out laughing and clapped him on his braided shoulder.

"Well, Stanislav," said he. "You'll have to do without a flight engineer. I expect you'll get by. What you've got to do is get out to the orbit of the equatorial satellite and wait for the 'Arrow'. The rest is up to the captain of the 'Arrow'."

Pishta, stunned, said nothing for several seconds. Then he understood.

"What're you doing?" he said softly, searching Gorbovsky's face. "Just what d'you mean? You're a spacer, what're you doing making gestures like this?"

"Gestures?" said Gorbovsky. "I don't know how. You go. You'll be responsible for them all to the end." He turned to the seniors: "March on board!" he shouted. "You go first or you'll never squeeze through,"—this to Pishta.

Pishta looked at the grim faces of the seniors, slowly wandering up the gangway, looked at the hatchway and the faces of the children peeping out, pecked Gorbovsky awkwardly on the cheek, nodded to Mark and Dixon, and raising himself on tiptoe grabbed hold of the brackets. Gorbovsky supported him from below.

The seniors with deliberate slowness began to press inside, shouting courageously: "Now then move up! Stiff upper lip! Who's howling over there? Heads up!" The last to go in was the same girl in the track suit. For a second she turned and looked hopefully at Gorbovsky. His face was stony.

"Can't get in," she said softly. "See, there's no room."

"You'll get thinner," promised Gorbovsky and taking her by the shoulders pushed her carefully into the crowd. He turned to Dixon:

"Where's the film?"

"Everything's taken care of," answered Percy weightily. "The picture comes on as soon as the ship blasts off. Children love surprises."

"Pishta!" cried Gorbovsky. "You ready?"

"Ready!" came the muffled reply.

"Start her, Pishta! Close the hatches! Good plasma, boys and girls!"

The heavy slab of the hatch moved noiselessly from its groove in the fuselage. Gorbovsky, in the midst of waving good-bye and stepping back from the coaming, suddenly remembered.

"A, the letter!" he exclaimed.

It wasn't in his breast pocket or in his trousers. The hatch was closing. For some reason the letter turned out to be in his inside pocket. Gorbovsky hastily thrust it onto the girl in the track suit and pulled his hand away fast. The hatch closed. He ran his hand along the metal, without himself quite knowing why; he looked at nobody as he descended, and Dixon and Mark dragged the steps away. There were only a few people left around the ship now while in the sky above cruised scores of helicopters and flyers.

Gorbovsky avoided the heap of valuables, stumbled over a bust of somebody and made his way round the ship to the passenger port, where Zhenya Vyazanitsyna was supposed to be waiting for him. I wish Matvei could have come, he thought gloomily. He felt squeezed dry and was very glad to see Matvei. Matvei was coming towards him, but he was alone.

"Where's Zhenya, then?"

Matvei stopped and looked about him. There was no sign of her.

"She was here," he said. "I was talking to her on the radiophone. Hatches closed already, eh?" He was still looking round.

"Yes, they'll be starting in a minute." He also cast his eyes about. Maybe she's in one of the helicopters, he thought. But he knew it was impossible.

"It's odd she isn't here," repeated Matvei.

"She may be in one of the helicopters," said Gorbovsky. He had suddenly realized where she was. Trust her, he thought.

"I didn't get to see Alyosha after all," said Matvei.

A strange welling sound, something like a throbbing sigh, rose over the spaceport. The huge blue mass of the ship noiselessly tore itself from the ground and slowly moved upwards. First time in my life I've seen my own ship

140

take off, thought Gorbovsky. Matvei was following the ship with his eyes, and suddenly, as if stung, turned on Gorbovsky and stared at him.

"Wait a minute..." he mumbled. "What're you doing here? Why... and the ship?"

"Pishta's in there," said Gorbovsky.

Matvei's eyes came to rest.

"There it is," he whispered.

Gorbovsky turned round. Above the horizon an even band of light was glaring, dazzlingly bright.

10

On the outskirts of the Capital Gorbovsky asked to stop. Dixon braked and looked expectantly at him.

"I'll walk it," said Gorbovsky.

He got out. Mark was right behind him, helping Alya Postysheva to get down. All the way from the port the two had sat without talking on the back seat, holding hands tight like children; Alya, her eyes closed, had sat with her face pressed into Mark's shoulder.

"Come with us, Percy," said Gorbovsky. "We'll pick some flowers and it's quite cool now. It'll be good for your heart."

"No, Leonid, let's say good-bye now. I'll drive on."

The sun was hanging just above the horizon. It was cool. The sun was shining as if in a corridor with black walls: the two Waves—the northern and the southern—were now high above the horizon.

"Along that corridor, look, follow my nose. Good-bye, Leonid, good-bye, Mark. And you miss, good-bye. Off you go . . . first I'm going to try for the last time to guess what you're going to do now. It's pretty easy at that."

"Yes, it's easy," said Mark. "Good-bye, Percy. Let's go."

Smiling briefly at Gorbovsky, he put his arm round Alya's shoulders and they walked off into the steppe. Gorbovsky and Dixon watched them go.

"A bit late," said Dixon.

"Yes," agreed Gorbovsky. "I envy them all the same."

"You love envying people, don't you? You always envy so richly, Leonid. I'm jealous as well. I'm jealous because somebody'll be thinking of him in his last moments, but about me . . . or you, Leonid, nobody."

"You want me to think of you?" asked Gorbovsky seriously.

"No, it's not worth it." Dixon screwed up his eyes looking at the declining sun. "Yes," he said. "This time, it seems, we're stuck. Good-bye, Leonid!"

He nodded and was gone, while Gorbovsky walked slowly along the highroad, along with other people, likewise wandering unhurriedly in the direction of the town. He felt calm and light for the first time on that confused, tense and terrible day. Nobody to worry about any more, no decisions to take, everybody around him was independent and he had become so himself. He had never been so independent in his life.

The evening was a fine one and if it had not been for the black walls to right and left, growing slowly into the blue sky, it would have been simply beautiful; quiet and clear, just the right degree of coolness, shot through by the slanting, pink rays of the sun. The number of people on the road dwindled; a lot of them went off into the steppe like Falkenstein and Alya, others stayed right there, by the roadside.

Along the main street of the town, pictures made multicoloured splashes as artists exhibited them for the last time—on trees, house walls, on the aqueducts across the road, on the columns of the energy grid. People stood in front of the pictures, reminiscing, possessed by a quiet joy, one tireless individual had even started an argument, while a good-looking thin woman was crying bitterly, repeating loudly: "A pity... such a pity!" Gorbovsky thought he had seen her somewhere before, but he couldn't remember exactly where.

Some unfamiliar music could be heard: in the open café next to the Council building a small wiry man was playing on a concert choriola with extraordinary passion and verve. People were sitting at the tables, listening to him with rapt attention; a lot more people were sitting listening on the steps and on the lawns in front of the café. The choriola

143

had a big piece of cardboard leaning against it, the legend in curving letters stated: **"Far Rainbow.** A song. Unfin."

There were a lot of people around the shaft and they were all busy. The huge dome of the entrance caisson, still incomplete, glinted dully. A chain of null-physicists, all carrying briefcases, parcels and piles of boxes led back into the theatre. Gorbovsky thought at once of the briefcase Malayev had given him. He tried to remember where he'd put it. Left it in the control room, most likely. Or was it in the hatch? What was the point of remembering anyway? He ought to be completely carefree. Odd, surely the physicists weren't still hoping? Of course you could always hope for a miracle. But it was amusing that the most sceptical and logical men on the planet were now relying on a miracle.

By the wall of the Council building a fellow in a ragged pilot's suit was sitting with his legs stretched out before him. He was blind and there was a bandage round his face. On his knees lay a shining nickel-plated banjo. His head thrown back, he was singing **Far Rainbow.**

The fake navigator, Hans, appeared from behind the dome carrying a huge bale on his shoulders. Catching sight of Gorbovsky, he broke into a smile and asked without stopping:

"Ah, captain! How's your ulmotrons? Did you get any? We're burying our records just now. It's a wearing business. A mad day it's been...." It seemed he was the only man on Rainbow who didn't know that Gorbovsky was the real captain of the "Tariel".

Matvei called to him from the window of the Council building.

"'Tariel' is in orbit already! They've just signed off. Everything's okay on board."

"Come on down," offered Gorbovsky. "Let's walk together."

144

Matvei shook his head.

"No, my friend," said he. "I've got loads to do and there's not a lot of time." He was silent for a moment, then added, wildly: "They've found Zhenya, you know where?"

"I can guess."

"Why did you do it?"

"I did nothing, honestly."

Matvei shook his head reproachfully and vanished back into the room.

Gorbovsky walked on and came out onto the sea shore, out onto the beautiful yellow beach with its many-coloured tents and comfortable deck chairs, with its boats drawn up alongside the low pier. He lowered himself into one of the deck chairs and stretched his legs in pleasure, folding his hands on his stomach; he looked steadily to the west, at the purple setting sun. To the right and to the left hung the black velvet walls, he tried not to notice them.

Right now I should have been starting for Lalanda, he thought as he drowsed. We would be sitting in the control room and I'd be telling them what a glorious planet Rainbow is and how I'd got round all of it in a day. Percy would say nothing, just sit twisting his beard in his fingers, Mark would be gruff and say it was all the old stuff, boring, the same as anywhere else. Tomorrow at this time we'd be coming out of deritrinitation. . . .

The beautiful girl with the grey in her golden hair, the one who had broken up his unpleasant conversation with Sklyarov at the spaceport just in time, walked past him, her head on her chest. She was walking along the very edge of the water and her face was no longer stony, It simply bore an endless weariness. About fifty yards from him she stopped and stood for a moment, looking at the sea; she sat down on the sand, resting her chin on her knees. Just then Gorbovsky became aware of a heavy sigh

145

by his ear and glancing up he saw Sklyarov. Sklyarov was also looking at the girl.

"What a meaningless farce," he said softly. "My life's been useless and the worst's been saved up for the last day...."

"Dear boy," said Gorbovsky. "What could be good about the last day?"

"You don't know...."

"Yes, I do. I know it all."

"You can't know everything ... I can hear the way you're talking to me."

"How?"

"Like to an ordinary man. But I'm a coward and a criminal."

"Now, Robert, what do you mean, you're a coward and a criminal?"

"I'm a coward and a criminal," repeated Robert stubbornly. "I'm worse than that probably, because I think I did right."

"There are no cowards and criminals," said Gorbovsky. "I'd as soon believe in a man rising from the dead as in one who could commit a crime."

"Stop trying to console me. I've told you, you don't know the whole story."

Gorbovsky lazily turned his head towards him.

"Robert," he said, "don't waste time. Go to her. Sit next to her.... I'm very comfortable here, but I'll help you if you want me to...."

"Nothing turns out the way you want it," said Robert gloomily. "I was certain I could save her. I thought I would do anything. It seems I couldn't. I'm going," he said suddenly.

Gorbovsky watched him walk away—at first strong and confident, then slower and slower, but he got there in the end and sat down beside her. She did not move away.

Gorbovsky watched them for a while trying to make out if he envied them or not, then dozed right off. He was awakened by the touch of something cold. He half opened one eye and saw Camille, his eternal absurd helmet, his eternal ascetic and gloomy face and his round unblinking eyes.

"I knew you were here, Leonid," he announced. "I've been looking for you."

"Hello, Camille," muttered Gorbovsky. "It's likely boring knowing everything."

Camille pulled up a deck chair and sat down beside him in the position of a man with a broken back.

"There're more boring things than that," he said. "I'm sick of it all. It was a big mistake."

"How are things in the next world?" asked Gorbovsky.

"It's dark there," said Camille. He fell silent. "Today I died and was resurrected three times. Each time it was terribly painful."

"Three times," repeated Gorbovsky. "A record." He looked at Camille. "Camille, tell me the truth. I've never understood. Are you human? Tell me. I shan't be able to tell anyone else now."

Camille thought for a moment.

"I don't know," he said. "I'm the last of the 'Baker's Dozen'. The experiment didn't work, Leonid. Instead of the feeling 'I want to but I can't' I have the feeling 'I can but I don't want to'. It's unbearable—to be able to and not to want to."

Gorbovsky was listening with his eyes shut.

"Yes, I understand," he said. "To be able to and not to want to, that's from the machine. And unbearable, that's from the man."

"You don't understand a thing," said Camille. "You like to think sometimes of the wisdom of the patriarchs, who had neither desires, nor feelings, nor even sensations. A mind

147

without flesh. The Great Logician. Logical methods demand absolute concentration. To do anything in science, day and night you have to think about one and the same thing, read about one and the same thing, talk about one and the same thing.... And where can you go from your psychic prism? Away from the inborn capacity to love.... You've got to love, read about love, you've got to have green hills, music, pictures, dissatisfaction, fear, envy.... You try to limit yourself—and you lose an enormous part of your happiness. And you know very well you're losing it. So then to blot out that consciousness and put an end to the torture of ambivalence, you castrate yourself. You tear away from yourself the whole emotional half of your humanity and you leave yourself with only one reaction to the world around you—doubt." Camille stopped. "Then loneliness lies in wait for you." With a terrible grief he looked at the evening sea, at the cooling beach, at the empty deck chairs throwing a strange triple shadow. "Loneliness..." he repeated. "You always kept away from me, you people. I was always superfluous, a bore, an incomprehensible eccentric. And now you're going. And I'll be left alone. Tonight I will rise from the dead for the fourth time alone on a dead planet, covered with ashes and snow...."

Suddenly the beach was noisy. The testers were descending towards the sea—eight testers, eight null-spacers who had never made it. Seven of them were carrying the eighth on their shoulders, he was blind, and his face was swathed in bandages. He had his head back and was playing his banjo, they were all singing:

> When up to the chest in trouble
>   Like dark water
>   You kept your head high
>   And looked for the crack of blue sky
>   And carried on....

Looking neither to right nor left, they marched singing into the sea up to their waist, chest, and then they swam after the setting sun holding their blind comrade on their backs. On the right of them was a black wall almost to the zenith, to the left a black wall almost to the zenith, only a thin dark-blue crack of sky remained, and the red sun, and the road of molten gold along which they swam and soon they were lost to view in the flash of the sun on the waves, and only the plink of the banjo could be heard and the song:

> ...You with head held high,
> Looked at the crack of blue
> And carried on....

www.ingramcontent.com/pod-product-compliance
Lightning Source LLC
Chambersburg PA
CBHW011406010726
47495CB00009B/2800